"AMANDA CROSS
mysteries are the kind one can recommend
wholeheartedly, not only to fans of the genre
but to people who never usually read mysteries
at all."
Publishers Weekly

"KATE FANSLER
is the treasure at the center of all Cross's cerebral
puzzles, intelligent, self-doubting, one of those rare
people who quote scores of writers unself-consciously
and to the point."
Newsweek

THE JAMES JOYCE MURDER
AMANDA CROSS
A Kate Fansler Mystery

THE
JAMES JOYCE
MURDER

Amanda Cross

BALLANTINE BOOKS • NEW YORK

Library of Congress Catalog Card Number: 67-11566

ISBN 0-345-30214-1

This edition published by arrangement with
The Macmillan Company

Manufactured in the United States of America

First Ballantine Books Edition: July 1982

To the first reader of this—and other things

Contents

Prologue

James Joyce's *Ulysses,* as almost everybody knows by now, is a long book recounting life in Dublin on a single day: June 16, 1904. It was on June 16, 1966, exactly sixty-two years later, that Kate Fansler set out for a meeting of the James Joyce Society, which annually held a "Bloomsday" celebration.

Adopting what she hoped was a properly Joycean attitude, Kate reminded herself that she would be approaching the Gotham Book Mart, home of the James Joyce Society, at almost the same hour in which Leopold Bloom, the hero of *Ulysses,* had walked out upon Sandymount Beach. "And had I any sense at all," Kate thought, "I would be on a beach myself." But having become temporary custodian of the Samuel Lingerwell papers, and thus unexpectedly involved in the literary correspondence of James Joyce, Kate thought it only proper that she attend tonight's celebration.

The Gotham Book Mart, on New York's West Forty-seventh Street, welcomes members of the James Joyce Society into a room at the rear of the shop. Kate was somewhat surprised to discover how many men were present—not only prominent Joyce scholars, but young men, the sort one least expected to encounter at the meetings of a literary society. But the reason was not far to seek. Writing their doctoral dissertations on Joyce, they hoped to come upon some secret, still undiscovered clue in the labyrinth of his works which would make their academic fortunes. For Joyce had by now, in the United States, added to all his other magic powers that of being able to bestow an academic reputation.

Kate was not a member of the James Joyce Society, but the name of Samuel Lingerwell assured her entrance, a welcome, a glass of the Swiss wine Joyce had especially favored. One thing is bloody certain, Kate thought after a time. When I pick a graduate student to help me with the Lingerwell papers, he will have to be most unJoycean, unLaurentian, unModern altogether. Someone who will not be searching for his own fortune among dear Sam's literary remains. On the whole, a Jane Austen devotee, I should imagine. Someone who calls her "Jane." I shall ask Grace Knole to recommend a likely candidate.

Which explains how Emmet Crawford came to spend the summer at Araby.

1

The Boarding House

"Kate," Reed Amhearst said, disentangling his long legs from the small car, "what on earth are you doing here? If you had decided to embrace the rural life, you might, in decency, have let me know. It's a great shock to return from Europe and find you established on some deserted hilltop in the Berkshires. What is the matter with that cow?"

Before Kate could answer, a red cat tore around the corner of the house with a brown dog in hot pursuit. "More of the local fauna," Kate said, in what she hoped were conciliatory tones. "Come inside and tell me all about New Scotland Yard. The cow is bellowing for her calf."

"Has she lost it?"

"It was taken away from her; she'll forget it in a day or two. How was England?"

Reed followed Kate into the huge vaulted living room, at one end of which chairs were grouped about a large fire. What certainly looked like a bar stood close by. Reed was proceeding toward the fireplace in a decorous manner when, from a nearby stairway he had not noticed, there burst as though catapulted into their midst a smallish boy. Reed pondered the possibilities of catapulting him back, and reluctantly dismissed them.

"See if you can answer this," the smallish male creature said, ignoring Reed. "Which is faster, bleeding to death or suffocating?"

"Suffocating, I should think," Kate ventured. Reed stared in fascination.

"You're wrong, wrong, wrong. I knew you'd be. Just remember this." The boy's gestures at this point indicated that Reed, too, might benefit from his advice. "If one man is drowning, and another is bleeding from a severed artery, work on the bleeding man first. It takes nine minutes longer to die from lack of oxygen than to bleed to death. How'd you like to shoot a few foul shots, Kate?"

"At the moment I'm engaged." Kate said. "Where is William?"

"Arguing with Emmet about some guy called James Joyce."

"Well, tell William to stop arguing about James Joyce and shoot some fouls with you. I take it today's essay is complete?"

"O.K., I'll get William," the boy returned, departing with an alacrity that suggested an unwillingness to dwell upon the subject of today's essay.

"Kate . . ." Reed began.

"Sit you down," Kate said. "Let me get you a drink and try to explain the whole thing."

"I've only come for a few days," Reed told her, accepting the chair. "This sounds as though it might carry us through to next Groundhog Day. Why didn't you tell me you were moving to the country? Who is that boy? Who is William? Who is Emmet? Not to mention the maternally stricken cow, the fiery cat and the pursuing dog. And who is James Joyce?"

"Certainly you know who James Joyce is?"

"If you mean the Irish author of several indecipherable books, I know who he is. But given the extraordinary aspects of this establishment, he might be the gardener. For God's sake, sit down and explain. I return from only six months in England to find you transformed, transported and transfigured."

"You just added that last one to make the series come out right."

"I certainly never expected to see you living in the same house with a small boy. What ages are Emmet and William?" Reed asked, as though suddenly struck with the awful thought that Kate had undertaken the housing of small boys in large numbers.

"In their middle or late twenties, I suppose. William Lenehan is tutoring Leo, he of the various deaths, and Emmet Crawford is going over some papers for me. The cat belongs to Emmet, and the dog belongs to the gardener, whose name is not James Joyce but Mr. Pasquale. The cow belongs to the farmer down the road who uses our land. Leo is my nephew. Cheers."

"Well, despite a three-hour drive I had not anticipated, and surroundings I could not have imagined, it's good to see you, Kate."

"And you. In the present circumstances, I might even risk hyperbole and say you're a sight for sore eyes."

"You're tired of all those cows; I'm not even complimented. I've missed you, Kate. In England I kept thinking . . ."

"Kate," interrupted a young man from the doorway. "If that woman is permitted entrance into this house, I shall have to tender my resignation. Reluctantly, to be sure, since the collection is a fascinating one. There's a letter—But I cannot have that woman hanging over me as though I were a pie and some extravagantly exciting news about you were the plum she was in hopes of pulling forth."

"Emmet, you must realize that country people are incurably curious, like cats. It's only urbanites who can ignore their neighbors. Tell Mrs. Bradford Leo is my illegitimate child, that I murdered his father, and that I'm setting up a polyandrous colony here in the hope of starting a new religion. That ought to keep her quiet for a while."

"The only thing that would keep that woman quiet is a bullet in the brain, and even then I'd think her lips would go on moving out of sheer force of habit. Her excuse for being here, incidentally, is to borrow some vinegar."

"Can't Mrs. Monzoni lend her some vinegar?"

"Mrs. Monzoni wouldn't lend Mary Bradford a wet paper towel. You had better go and cope. Why not tell her I've just served ten years for cannibalism, and am not to be trusted when aroused?"

"Oh, very well. Reed, may I introduce Emmet Crawford. Mr. Reed Amhearst." Kate departed with evident reluctance, followed by the palpable sympathy of Emmet.

"Who is Mrs. Monzoni?" Reed asked.

"The cook. Have you read the correspondence Joyce had with his English publishers in 1908? It's enough to make a cat cry. Imagine thinking *Dubliners* obscene because it suggested that Edward VII was less than a paragon of virtue, and used the word 'bloody' on two occasions. Of course, Lingerwell changed all that, bless his courageous heart. He also did the *Portrait* and the *Rainbow*."

"Do you mean he was a painter?"

"Who?"

"Lingerwell."

"A painter? Why on earth should a painter publish the *Portrait?*"

"I can't imagine. Mr. Crawford, I have the unhappy sense of not having understood a single circumstance or statement since I first drove up that unduly precipitous hill . . ."

"I bet it's something in winter . . ."

"To be frank, I have no interest in its condition during either the temperate or intemperate seasons. I am trying to understand what you're talking about. How does one *do* a *Rainbow?*"

"Aren't you from the Library of Congress?"

"Certainly not. I am from the office of the district

attorney of the County of New York, if my profession happens to be germane to this extraordinary discussion."

"Sorry. The Library of Congress people have been rather camping on our doorstep. Have you come to make an arrest?"

"I have come, I had hoped I had come, to pay a visit. I am a friend of Miss Fansler's."

"That will be nice for Kate. William and I do rather stick to hermeneutics, theological and nontheological, and Leo's conversation alternates between basketball and the grimmer aspects of first aid. Well, perhaps I may assume the departure of Mary Bradford and return to my Odyssean labors. See you at dinner." He wandered out to leave Reed balancing the relative advantages of another drink and an immediate departure. With the return of Kate, the scales tilted decidedly toward the drink.

"She's gone," Kate said, "though not without collecting a bottle of vinegar, expressing inchoate horror at the use of wine vinegar at twice the price of ordinary, asking if she could borrow the house for her garden club's tea, informing me she was busier than anyone else on earth, and wondering, with barely concealed salaciousness, what were the functions of the two young men in this household. I have become very disillusioned about the rural character. I suspect that Wordsworth, when he took to the country, never spoke to anyone but Dorothy and Coleridge, and perhaps an occasional leech gatherer. Tell me about England."

"Kate! *What are you doing here?*"

At that moment there arose from outside the cry as of a pack of wolves about to make the kill. "I forbear to ask what that is," Reed said wearily.

"I expect," Kate said, walking in a leisurely fashion to the window, "that is the Araby Boys' Camp arriving for a wienie roast. Reed, would you like to take me to dinner at a not very reputable hash-joint-cum-bar in a nearby town? I warn you that they play the juke-box constantly, but the surroundings might be more easily ignored."

"I never dreamed," Reed said, leading Kate firmly from the room, "that I would look forward to a juke-box as to the Sirens singing." Reed closed the Volks-wagen door on Kate, walked round to the driver's side, and again folded his long legs in place beneath the steering wheel. He turned the tiny car around and burst down the driveway so precipitously that Kate could well imagine the look of admiration directed at their back by numberless awestruck boys.

"Why have you set up a boarding house?" Reed asked, when they were seated in the booth. "When I left you, you were a more or less rational associate professor of English. Have you lost your senses, your money or your grip? I have seldom been so alarmed about anyone."

"It's not *really* a boarding house, of course, it just looks that way at a superficial glance. Actually, my whole summer situation can be summed up as a for-tuitous concatenation of improbable events. Which is to say that life has this in common with prizefighting: if you've received a belly blow, it's likely to be fol-lowed by a right to the jaw."

"I didn't know you were fond of boys."

"I am *not* fond of boys. If you mean Leo, he is the right to the jaw. The point is, Reed, you simply weren't here when I got around to the thought of consulting you. Surely there's enough crime in New York without your rocketing off to England."

"England has gone a long way toward solving the problem of crime caused by drug addiction. They have *not* gone a long way toward solving the problem of ec-centric behavior—in fact, I think they invented it. If Leo is the right to the jaw, may we begin by discuss-ing, according to your exceedingly ill-informed and inappropriate figure from prizefighting, the belly blow?"

"I don't think you knew Sam Lingerwell—I'll have the veal cutlets and spaghetti; I wouldn't exactly *rec-*

ommend it, but it's distinctly superior to the chicken pie."

"Two veal cutlets and spaghetti," Reed told the waitress. "I heard of Mr. Lingerwell for the first time this afternoon; he was mentioned by Emmet Crawford in the midst of some extraordinary story about Edinburgh."

"Dublin, surely. James Joyce."

"You're right. Dublin. Curiouser and curiouser."

"Sam Lingerwell died last fall, at the ripe and wonderful age of ninety. He sat down in a chair, lit up a cigar, and started to read a book by Sylvia Townsend Warner. They found him in the morning. I went to school with Lingerwell's daughter, and in some way I continued to be friends with him and his wife long after his daughter joined a convent."

"A convent?"

"I'll come to that part of the story in a moment. Sam, and the Calypso Press which he started—well, you've got to read some of Alfred Knopf's memoirs of publishing in his early days to know what I mean. Sam was one of the grand old men of publishing; there are scarcely any of them left. The sort who knew literature, had guts, and would have thought you were hallucinating had you mentioned the present tribal customs of Madison Avenue. They all went back to a time when it was possible to go into the publishing business without a million dollars, a taste for cocktails, a publicity manager and fourteen computers. All right, I'll spare you the speech about the good old days. Suffice it to say, Sam was the best there was, and in those days that was pretty good. He was the American publisher who had the guts, the taste or whatever it took to publish James Joyce and D. H. Lawrence and lots of others, English and American, whom we now consider classics, but who were just thought to be dirty naturalists back around the First World War."

"Ah, I begin to understand what 'rainbow' Mr. Crawford and I were discussing."

"The *Rainbow* was later, of course, but I'm glad to hear you're getting the idea. At the moment, we're all thinking more about Joyce. Emmet, with occasional grunts of encouragement from me, is trying to sort out Sam's letters by author, so that we can decide whose correspondence ought to go where, which may explain why Dublin keeps coming up in the conversation. *Dubliners* was the first book of Joyce's anybody published. Now don't let me wander on to Joyce; one just keeps going, getting more and more complicated with each sentence and never arriving at any conclusion. Where was I?"

"The good old days of publishing."

"Ah, yes. Well, Sam had been publishing marvelous books and corresponding with now famous authors for something like fifty years, and needless to say he'd accumulated quite a valuable library and collection of papers. In recent years he'd let people use some of the letters he could get his hands on for collections and so forth, but it was clear that something had to be done to organize his papers and library, so—two years ago he purchased the house in which you were so shocked to find me today, moved all his literary and other belongings up here, and prepared to follow in due course. In the meantime, he traveled. I doubt, really, that he would ever have moved up here. Sam liked to joke about what he would do in his 'old age.' "

"Where was his wife?"

"She died a number of years ago. Sam had a fine life, friends, interesting occasions and good conversation, but his family life was a sad one. He and his wife had two daughters; one died of cancer in her early twenties, and the other, Veronica, the one I went to school with, became a nun. Sam was an agnostic humanist, like most of the intellectuals of his generation, and her conversion and all was a great blow to him. Still he saw her from time to time and they were on good terms. Sam left everything to Veronica in his will, including the house."

"How did *you* get involved in all this?"

"That *is* the point, I do realize that. I'm sorry this explanation is so long, particularly since, once you understand the background to the story, it doesn't become a bit more intelligible, really. As I said, Sam died. He didn't have a funeral, not believing in these matters. The *Times* obituary mentioned Veronica's convent, and I wrote her a note. A short while later I had a reply, and she asked to come and see me."

"Bringing with her an eight-year-old boy named Leo whom she had acquired at the nearest orphanage."

"Reed, you're not paying attention. I told you Leo was my nephew. There is no connection between Leo and Veronica."

"Of course not. Silly of me to have thought it. Do we risk the blueberry pie or just settle for coffee? Good. Veronica, you were saying, came to see you."

"There's no need to tell you this if you're going to be petulant."

"I petulant? I have the world's sweetest disposition, as who knows better than you. It is only that, as I motored up here in my little Volkswagen, I pictured talking to you by the fire in peace and quiet, instead of which I find you in the midst of a positive holocaust of male activity. Do you suppose if we went back now the fireside would be deserted? At least all those dreadful boys may have shrieked their way off into the night, stuffed with wienies."

"Reed, don't you care for children?"

"Not in the least."

"Odd, I never knew that."

"I would have told you, as the maid said when resigning from the house where they kept alligators, but I didn't think the question would come up."

"Well, well. I'm afraid my hearth will not yet be sufficiently deserted. Shall we take a walk?"

"Since I don't appear to have a choice in the matter, I acquiesce with my usual grace." Reed paid the bill, and they walked into the evening. "Do continue," Reed said. "Veronica came to see you . . ."

"Yes. She explained that her father had left all his possessions including his library and papers, and the 'boarding house,' as you call it, to her—and would I help her to determine exactly what *was* in the collection so that it might be best disposed of. I pointed out that someone who knew the market value of these things would be more to the point, but it seems she's not interested in money, but in getting the books and papers to the places where they will do the most good. She had already been besieged by universities, the Library of Congress, and so forth and so on."

"Was there any particular reason why she should come to you?"

"No reason, or—if your mind happens to work that way—every reason. I knew and loved her father, who had gone out of his way to be kind to me on many occasions; I think she understood that I would welcome a chance to serve him, even posthumously. There aren't, I suppose, many people who realize that to provide an opportunity for service may be in itself a service. Do you follow me?"

"Exactly, as you know."

"Also, there weren't really all that many people she could go to. All she suggested, of course, was that I take a couple of days to look through things—families with collections of papers rarely have a clue as to the work involved in sorting them out. You know about the Boswell papers found in a croquet box in an old castle?" Reed shook his head.

"Remind me to tell you, the next conversation but one. It became clear that the collection ought to be sorted, and that it would take more than just me to do it. I began, in the vaguest way, to fool with the idea of spending the summer here instead of dancing off to Europe."

"I begin to see, as through a glass darkly."

"A cloud no bigger than a man's hand. That cloud was soon joined by another, Leo."

"I wait, ears eagerly attuned, for an explanation of Leo. To be frank, I have never fathomed the mystery of your familial connections."

"Familial connections are always difficult to explain, and impossible to sever. Not that one really wants to, I suppose. However trying one's family, there is some call of blood to blood which one is somehow impelled to answer. I have nothing in common with any member of my family, and yet in crisis, personal or national, one always rallies round."

"What is a national crisis?"

"Christmas."

"Oh, I see."

"This crisis, however, was personal. Leo is the middle one of three children, and apparently all middle children exist precariously upon the earth, threatened from above and below, so to speak, and trembling with insecurity, which often takes the form of obstinance, violence and pure laziness. I don't claim to understand why, if you can be beautifully secure thinking of yourself as an older child, or a younger child, you can't say to yourself 'I am the middle child' and go on to something else, but then child psychology has always been beyond me. In any event, Leo was doing poorly at school, badly at home, and indifferently at Group."

"Group?"

"Reed, I really think you're *trying* to be perverse. Surely you know what Group is—didn't you go to one on Saturdays when you were a little boy in New York?"

"I was *not* a little boy in New York. I was a little boy in Baltimore, Maryland."

"Oh. A backward community, obviously. Groups are to knit up the loose ends of offsprings' hours when parents might otherwise go mad. For a walloping sum, Group takes your child to the park, ice skating, or climbing on the Palisades. Leo did not care for Group. Personally, I see this as a sign of clear intellectual ability, but Leo's parents, and the child guidance counselor they consulted, looked on it in a different light.

"All this, of course, would have had nothing in the world to do with me," Kate continued, "if fate, which the Greeks understood so well and we so poorly, had not taken a hand. Leo's parents decided to give a family dinner party to celebrate their wedding anniversary, and in an unfortunate moment of familial sen-

timentality, I consented to attend. All three of my
brothers are constantly trying to draw me into their
various social circles, though they have, thank God,
rather given up introducing me to socially acceptable
bachelors. I'm getting older, the bachelors are becoming more inveterate in their bachelorhood, and anyway I can never be trusted to behave properly. Leo's
father is the youngest brother. Reed! What an angel
you are to listen to all this. The truth is, I guess, I've
been rather lacking a sympathetic ear."

"Is this youngest brother as stuffy as the rest?"

"Stuffier. But he's also the one who invests money
for me, and helps me with my income tax, so I've
developed more of a modus vivendi with him than with
the others. What possessed me, at the night of their
anniversary dinner, to mention Sam Lingerwell and his
library and his house in the country, I cannot imagine.
True, I was graveled for lack of matter in conversation
there, as always, but I am still inclined to blame the
gods. However, the fact that I might be spending the
summer in the country implanted itself in the not particularly fervent imagination of my brother, and a
week later I got an invitation to lunch.

"This in itself," Kate said, stopping to light a cigarette, and perching herself uncertainly on a tree
stump, "was ominous. He said he had a favor to ask
of me, and hoped I would lunch with him at White's,
where they serve Beefeater martinis for which, he remembered, I had a fondness. It would never occur to
my brother to come uptown and have lunch at a place
convenient for me. Favor or no favor, he works and
I—well, he has never really faced the fact that I work,
and anyway, what do professors *do?* With my usual
dexterity, I leapt to the conclusion that it was a
question of money. It has always bothered my brother
that although I inherited exactly as much money as
he did, I have been content to live off the income, and
let my stocks grow, or divide, or whatever it is stocks
are always doing. As long as I never actually touched
my capital, my brother couldn't really complain if I
wasn't trying as hard as I ought to be to double my

portfolio or turn over my investments or any of those obscure financial operations. But I thought, well, probably he's gone and discovered he needs a little ready cash, and he's going to try to negotiate some complicated thing. I went, prepared to have two martinis and to extract every ounce of satisfaction from his monetary problems.

"I couldn't have been more wrong." Kate made a little hole in the earth and buried her cigarette end. "My brother is very rich indeed, and probably would have been startled to death to know I'd even thought he would be interested in my slender funds. He, needless to say, has doubled *his* inheritance many times over, as well as earning all sorts of money in that Wall Street law firm of his. It transpired, when I was barely through my first martini, that he wanted to talk about Leo.

"What it all came down to was that Leo was behind in school, recalcitrant when he wasn't aggressive, and he needed a summer devoted to being tutored, *not* being sent away to a camp, and living in a household of which he would be a single juvenile member. In short, my brother, putting together Leo's problems, the advice from the guidance counselor, and my unfortunate confidence about my summer plans, suggested that I take Leo for the summer, complete with tutor, give him that sort of 'I take you for granted and like you just as you are' treatment which appears to be my manner with children—the truth is, if forced to talk to children, I talk to them exactly as I talk to anyone else—and see if we might get Leo back on the rails. My brother had promised to take his wife to Europe for the summer, and I gathered, without exactly being told, that any disappointment in this matter would be likely to render my brother's life uncomfortable for a considerable period of time. He offered to pay for the tutor, whom I would hire, to lend me his elegant car, and to bear the expenses of the whole 'boarding house' operation."

"So you agreed?"

"Of course not. I absolutely declined. I told my

brother that he and his wife could jolly well take a house themselves and minister to Leo. I finished my two Beefeater martinis, my lunch, capped it off with an excellent brandy, and departed in a cloud of righteous indignation."

"Kate," Reed said, "you are the most maddening woman I have ever met. I can't imagine, for example, why I, who could be happily resting in an air-conditioned apartment in New York, should be walking along a country road with you, being devoured by mosquitoes and uncomfortably aware, from the tickling in my nose, that I am about to begin a prolonged attack of hay fever."

"One doesn't get hay fever in July."

"Well, whatever one gets in July, I'm getting. There! You see." Reed sneezed violently. "Yet here I am, slapping at mosquitoes, hating the country, and an exile from even such house as you have in it. How did you end up with Leo, for God's holy sake?"

"He ran away and came to me. It became quite clear that everyone was trying so hard to understand him that he longed to be in the company of someone who didn't understand him and wouldn't even try. I sent him back home, of course, but I promised he might spend the summer with me. My brother, with the mulishness that marks all simple-minded people, was outraged that Leo should have run away to me. Anyhow, that's how the 'boarding house' came so overwhelmingly into existence."

2

An Encounter

Reed, who had fallen into what fitful sleep he could find between the discomforts of mosquito bites, sneezing and confusion, was awakened the next morning by a boy's voice saying, quite distinctly, almost it seemed in his ear: "Hurray! I got the bitch, I'm sure I did!" This was followed by an older voice answering in stern tones: "You must *not* use the word 'bitch.' As I have tried to explain, there is language one uses with one's associates, and language one uses with one's elders, and these overlap only about fifty percent of the time. 'Bitch' is *not* an incidence of overlapping, except when applied to the female of the canine species. But," the voice added, in lower tones, "I do believe you nailed her."

Reed sat up in bed. Probably it was a dream. He found his watch on the night table and consulted it: five forty-five. Impossible. Yet the second hand of his grandfather's excellent watch continued to plod its way round its small dial. This was it, the absolute, unarguable end. He would climb into his car and be gone as soon as he could capture a cup of coffee, Kate or

25

no Kate. However fond he was of Kate, there were experiences he was not prepared to undergo. Kate— Reed lay back for a moment and thought about Kate. A shout from some female in what seemed the throes of a temper tantrum could be heard at a certain distance. Not Kate: an unpleasant voice. Kate's voice . . . Reed was asleep.

When he awoke again his grandfather's watch said ten minutes to ten, and all was golden silence. Perversely, he wondered what had happened to everybody. Dressed, he tiptoed into the living room: deserted. No one burst into the room or catapulted down the steps. Relaxing slightly, Reed moved on into the dining room, where he found a place set, with a sign saying "For you" sitting neatly on the plate. A glass of orange juice stood on the sideboard in a bowl of chopped ice; next to it stood an electric coffeepot, a toaster, some bread and a box of cold cereal. Propped against the cereal was a sign saying "No eggs served after nine-thirty." Grinning, Reed carried his orange juice to the table and picked up the newspaper lying by his plate. A newspaper in the country! Imagine! His astonishment turned to bemusement as he noticed it was yesterday's *Berkshire Eagle*. On it Kate had written: "In case reading a paper at breakfast is a necessity." Reed settled down to the *Berkshire Eagle*.

The silence of the household persisted through breakfast and followed him out onto the lawn. It was one of those days, Reed decided, when even the person most persistently skeptical of rural charms succumbs to the conviction that the creation of the earth was not an absolute nonsense. A hummingbird, apparently motionless in midair, darted from flower to flower. Reed gazed happily about him.

The guest room in which he had spent the night looked out over the back of the house; a fence, with a gate in it, ran perhaps six feet from his window. The voices he had overheard must have been leaning on the gate. Who, Reed, wondered, was the bitch they had "got"? Turning from the gate, he followed a path which led to a driveway and thence to a road. He would take a walk. He paused in the road to light his pipe and muse on the peace of rural life. Apart from the telephone poles and electric wires nothing had changed, he was certain, in a hundred years. On a distant hillside, cows moved in the sunlight. Reed decided he quite liked cows forming part of the landscape on a distant hillside. Puffing at his pipe, he thrust his hands in his pockets and started down the road. Any illusions he might have had about a rural universe untouched by the industrial revolution were immediately shattered by four simultaneous uproars. First he heard the roar of jet engines, and, looking up, saw the white trail of what was probably the eleven o'clock jet from Boston to Chicago. On the road an old jalopy roared by, apparently with a souped-up engine, going, Reed was prepared to swear, eighty miles an hour, and driven, to judge from the glimpse he managed to get, by an adolescent whose arrogance, together with his engine's exhaust, floated out behind the car in a general pollution of the atmosphere. On a field to Reed's left, a tractor started up, and down the road from him a giant milk truck performed some mechanized maneuver. Reed retreated into the driveway.

Perhaps on the whole it would be better to go through the gate and down across the fields. He unlatched the gate, walked through it, latched it again (for the field was clearly for cows, though none were presently inhabiting it), and started to stroll. He was immediately joined by the large brown dog, but its aim seemed companionship rather than violence. Reed again lit his pipe, thrust his hands into his pockets, and stepped forward into an enormous mound of fresh cow dung.

His remarks, happily audible to none but the brown dog, were certainly such as might have been heard on the countryside a hundred years ago, perhaps on a similar occasion. Some aspects of rural life were clearly unchanged. These did not, however, include the extraordinary machine which, headed in Reed's direction across a field of hay, seemed to be making the most frightful clatter and flinging huge objects into the air. With a shrug indicating that he would have to throw out the shoes in any case, Reed set off across the fields in the direction of the machine. The dog, who considered that some union had been consummated by the occasion of Reed's swearing, trotted along.

Together man and dog approached the machine, which seemed, with some amazing mechanical awareness, to have seen them coming and to have paused in its flinging operations. As they approached, however, Reed could determine that if mechanization had reached farming, automation had not: the machine was being pulled by a tractor, and the tractor was being driven by a man. He awaited Reed's approach in an attitude of pleasant anticipation.

"Stepped in it, eh?" he asked when Reed was within earshot.

"Could you see all the way from there?"

"Just could tell by the way you hopped about. Visiting Miss Fansler?"

"Temporarily," Reed answered, amused to see that curiosity extended to the males hereabouts. It occurred to him that this might be the husband of the disliked Mary Bradford who came to borrow vinegar.

"My name's Bradford," the man on the tractor said, in confirmation of this thought.

"Amhearst," Reed answered.

"That's the name of the town where I went to college," Bradford said. "U. Mass. Agricultural School. Are you surprised that a farmer went to college?"

"I am," Reed said frankly. "I thought farmers considered book learning nonsense."

"Those that do go broke. Farming's changed more in the last twenty years than in a thousand years before that."

"I can see that." Reed pointed to the baler.

"That is quite a machine," Bradford said. "It picks up the hay, pushes it through that machine there, which binds it into bales and wraps them with string, and then tosses the bales into that wagon. When the wagon's full, I use my other tractor to pull it back to the barn, where the bales are put on an elevator which carries them to the hayloft."

"What do you do if the machine breaks down?"

"Fix it. A farmer who can't fix his own machinery is in trouble. Want to see this thing work? Hop up."

This seemed to Reed, who was absolutely nonathletic, like an invitation to commit suicide. But Bradford pointed to the rod connecting the tractor with the baler, expecting Reed to stand on that. Reed complied.

When they started off, Reed's attention was absorbed, first in holding on, and then in wondering how soon his teeth would be knocked out of his head. It was only after they had traversed the field several times that he managed to watch the baler: the hay had been previously cut and turned over to lie in rows. The baler scooped it up, bound it, tied it up, and spat it out. Amazing. The brown dog trotted alongside, appearing in imminent danger of being run over. But all these rural creatures had adapted to the machine as readily as they had adapted to the other changes in their environment. "Yet I," Reed thought, "am not adapting. In fact, I'll probably develop a permanent tremor."

Bradford finally stopped the machine as it appeared to be about to penetrate a barbed-wire fence; Reed, shaken into indifference, rather hoped it would. But Bradford handled his machine as though it were a horse whose spirit he admired. As Reed stepped down he greeted the earth, cow dung and all, with a silent prayer of exaltation. He had received and met some challenge during his ride on the baler. Reed lit his pipe.

"What did they use for baling when you were a boy?" he asked.

"Horses, a pitchfork, and three men, I guess," Bradford answered. "But I was a boy in Scarsdale and don't really know."

"Scarsdale!"

"Yes. My father was a lawyer. I like farming. My wife's from around here—her family swam over in

front of the Mayflower with the painter in their teeth.
Beautiful here, isn't it?" The last phrase bore no shade
of sarcasm. Reed followed Bradford's gaze. It was
beautiful. "It's most beautiful on a tractor, from the
middle of the fields. Come for another ride someday."
Bradford waved his hand and started up the tractor.
Reed walked back across the field, trying first one
muscle and then another, in anticipation of the ache
he knew to be inevitable.

When he had shut the gate behind him, he saw
Kate, reading in a lounge chair under a tree. "Does
the schedule permit of conversation now?" he asked.

"It had better. Mary Bradford is on her way to
bring back the vinegar and partake of a cup of coffee."

"I, too," said Reed, collapsing into a chair, "have
had an encounter. With Mary Bradford's husband."

"I know that already, you urban innocent. Mary
Bradford saw you leap on the machinery, apparently
waited to see if your intentions were homicidal, and
determining that they weren't, decided to find out what
you had said to her husband before he got the chance
to tell her himself."

"You make her sound a most attractive lady. Has
she no redeeming features—salt of the earth, perhaps,
a natural bonhomie, a certain physical vigor?"

"Most of her physical vigor, as you shall soon hear,
is in her voice. To hear her tell it, nobody works
as hard as she, nobody contributes so much to society
and receives so little from it, nobody has so much
rectitude, propriety and good old-fashioned morality.
Since her golden rule is 'Do unto Mary Bradford as
Mary Bradford would like you to do unto her,' it is difficult to see whence her high moral tone. But don't
let me prejudice you. What did you talk about with
Brad?"

"As it happens, I was so busy having my teeth
shaken out of my head, and observing the wonders
of mechanized farming, that we didn't say very much.

My shoes are covered with cow dung, and my spirit is oppressed."

"Reed. Have we got you down with our noisy ways? As I hope you could see this morning, our household is not really as mad as it seemed yesterday. This *is* peaceful, isn't it?"

"All events have conspired to rob me of my self-respect. I left New York yesterday feeling rested, vigorous and able, in my own way, to cope. Ever since I chugged up your beastly driveway I have been reminded of my ignorance, dipped in cow dung, made to appear effete next to some sunburned monster of masculinity on a tractor, and finally doomed, it seems, to listen to the chatter of the sunburned monster's wife."

"You don't fool me for a minute," Kate said. "Your masculinity and self-respect are no more in danger from today's events than they have ever been. You may be suffering from a surplus of fresh air—I know the feeling. Reed, I think what I cherish most about you is that calm assurance that does not need to prove itself. As to the cow dung, although it may be ruining a good pair of shoes, its price is above rubies and the envy of all gardeners. Pasquale will scrape it off your shoes and put it around a flower."

"Kate, the truth of the matter is, I had rather hoped . . ." But the sudden entrance of a car into the driveway dashed the hope or left it unexpressed. "Do you mean she drove up from just down the road?" Reed asked in amazement.

"No one ever walks in the country, except city folk. Hardworking farmers have no time for such foolishness. Hello, Mary," Kate called, getting to her feet. "May I introduce Mr. Amhearst. Mrs. Bradford."

"I guessed it was you in the guest room this morning when I came to get the cows. You can always tell when there's someone in the guest room because the windows are open then, and the blinds down, which of course they aren't when the room's empty. Ah, I thought, Kate Fansler has another guest. I bet it's a young man, she prefers men guests. I prefer women, who make their beds and don't expect to be waited on hand and foot, but then Kate has all those servants, so that probably isn't a consideration with her—I do envy people with help, but of course they all want to be paid a fortune and not do a thing—that dreadful Mrs. Pasquale down the road came in to help me once, talking, talking all day long, and I ended up doing all the work myself. No point to that."

Reed, who had risen, scarcely knew which part of this diatribe to respond to, if, indeed, any response was necessary.

"I hear you're a district attorney," Mary Bradford said.

Reed now stared at her in total amazement. He caught Kate's eye and saw her shrug, a shrug which said, "I didn't tell her."

"Shall we go in the house and have a cup of coffee?" said Kate, moving firmly toward the door.

"I really shouldn't," Mary Bradford said, following her. "I've baskets of raspberries to make into jam, and these days, of course, I'm my own hired man; then, if I don't get to clean the upstairs soon, we'll simply have to move out of it, and Brad, of course, is worse than the children, throwing his clothes around—I always get a sock right up in the vacuum cleaner, 'Look,' I say, 'I'm not the only person around here capable of picking things up . . .'" Reed paused on the back porch to remove his shoes and socks and entered the house with bare feet. His normal impulse would have been to go to his room for another pair of shoes and socks, but the thought of allowing his naked feet to become grist to Mary Bradford's mill was too strong. He began to understand the effect Mary Bradford had on people. The woman positively tempted one to behave in an improper manner in order to provide her with material. This was an effect of undue propriety, shading off into prurience, which Reed had not personally observed before, and it fascinated him.

They settled themselves around the dining room table: everyone soon had a cup of coffee. Reed had the strange sensation of taking part in some aboriginal ritual. He wiggled his toes quite happily, and wondered what on earth Mary Bradford would find to say next.

"I call it shocking and improper behavior," she said, accepting one of Kate's cigarettes. "I've given up smoking," she added, lighting it. "Naturally, it's nobody's business what a man does in his own house, I suppose, but he rides up the road with them in a convertible, bold as you please, and what goes *on* in a big house like that on a weekend, all those girls. An orgy. I wouldn't be surprised," she added with a significant look, "if there were drugs. Drink of course goes without saying. One morning all those people are going to get up to do something, and find they can't stagger further than the nearest bottle."

"Are we discussing someone I know?" Reed asked in a voice straining so hard for innocence it sounded simpering to his own ears.

"The district attorney's office of Berkshire County ought to know about him," Mary Bradford said with emphasis. "But of course they haven't even got time to pick up these people who speed down the road, going fifty miles an hour right past a sign saying 'Children. Go Slow.' I have to lock my children in the house when the summer people come, I don't mind telling you."

"The boy I saw rocketing by this morning didn't look like 'summer people' to me," Reed said.

"That white trash," Mary Bradford snorted, identifying the car in question with no difficulty. "A new baby every year, and not enough sense or money to care for the ones they have. Who wouldn't have eighteen children if it weren't a question of buying them shoes?"

"How many do you have?" Reed asked. He was curious to discover if Mary Bradford ever stopped talking long enough to answer a question. Kate merely sat back, smiling. Clearly she had been through all this several times before.

"Two," Mary Bradford said. "And they're properly dressed and not allowed to run around picking up whatever they take a fancy to. Of course, once that camp opens and all those lazy parents who send their children to the day camp come rushing up the road, it's impossible to cross over to our barn safely. But then, we're just farmers, and no one worries about farmers. You have to learn how to go on welfare, or get some union to support you, to succeed these days. Well, I must get back and make Brad's lunch. He'll just have to have peanut butter sandwiches. With all those raspberries to do there isn't time to prepare anything." She talked her way out of the house and into her car, pausing to make statements and then to digress from them at extraordinary length until, when she had finally backed the car out, Reed felt that he had survived an air raid, and that someone ought to sound the all clear.

"What sort of meal," Reed asked, "is lunch around here? If you think you catch a note of trepidation in my voice, it is definitely there. Kate, my sweet, I long for you to return to civilization, and I shall hope to commandeer hours of your time when you do, but I am afraid that I'm too frail a being altogether to withstand the rigors of the rural life. I don't know which is more horrifying, really, being bounced about on a tractor, wallowing in manure, or listening to the conversation of that angel of light from down the road. Not only is she malicious and suffering from logorrhea, she doesn't even conclude a thought. Who is that sybaritic chap down the road with the girls and the orgies?"

Kate laughed, "A very amusing character, as it happens, who's coming to dinner tonight. He's stopped in several times with invitations, and I finally proffered one. Just as you insist on trotting around in your bare feet, giving Mary Bradford loads to say when next she shares a cup of coffee with a neighbor, so Mr. Mulligan goes out of his way to act like an inebriated playboy. As a matter of fact, I've talked with him long enough to gather that he's a full professor of English and has published a good many books of literary criticism. Please don't go, Reed. Stay at least until tomorrow, meet Mr. Mulligan, and let us try to restore your faith in the countryside. It has its charms, you know. Open fires, silence, long lonely walks, beauty that sometimes takes one's breath away."

"I noticed the beauty on my tractor ride. Would you care to take one of those lonely walks? As a matter of fact, I set one foot on the road this morning and was nearly run down by the industrial revolution."

"Let's take some sandwiches, which I promise will not be peanut butter, and have lunch at the top of that hill. The brown dog will probably accompany us, but otherwise it should be quite peaceful. Of course, Mary Bradford will undoubtedly see us go, and conclude The Worst."

"I shall look on it as a moral obligation to render one of Mary Bradford's suspicions correct. I feel quite inspired. All right, all right, I'm going to get on some shoes."

"And I shall get the sandwiches."

"Well," said Reed, "I am prepared to stay until tomorrow morning, reconsidering the possibilities of the rural life. I suppose Leo will join us for dinner?"

"And Emmet and William, but without the rest of the Araby Boys' Camp. Leo will report on The World, as passed by Mr. Artifoni, who runs the A.B.C., but otherwise, it won't be too absolutely terrible. Wait and see. Mr. Mulligan is nice, and Emmet really quite interesting in his effete, and William in his bluff, way."

"What I look forward to is spending the afternoon on the hills in my way. You don't suppose we'll meet herds of cows do you, or," he added, "a bull?"

"No bulls around here."

"Then whence the calves? Have they developed parthenogenesis?"

"They have developed artificial insemination."

"There is no doubt about it, country living is decadent, immoral and soul-annihilating. Does the brown dog have a name? We appear to have become friends."

"Brownie."

"And what is the name of the red cat?"

"Cassandra. She belongs to Emmet. But she is usually called Pussens."

"What was *that?*" Reed stopped with one foot on the porch.

"Someone shooting woodchucks."

"Do you think they are likely to shoot us by mistake?"

"Well, they have telescopic sights on the guns, and presumably they can tell us from a woodchuck."

"Kate."

"Yes."

"Hurry up and make those damn sandwiches. If we're going to be shot, let us die in one another's arms."

"We are going," Kate said, "for a walk."

"I wonder," Reed mused, "what Mary Bradford thinks goes on in a rural orgy. Well, at least I know that if you're drowning and bleeding to death all at once, I shall apply a tourniquet immediately and wait for the proper moment to begin artificial respiration. I must remember to ask Leo at dinner how long Mr. Artifoni says it takes to die of a bullet wound."

3

Counterparts

Reed and Kate sat at opposite ends of the dinner table; from time to time their eyes met, but for the most part they listened to the exchange between those on either side. It had been a good walk, a good afternoon. The cocktail hour had been, if not shattered, at least cracked by the return of Leo, but Reed did not feel inclined to complain. Kate seemed to treat the whole matter of Leo in the light of a fascinating experience, like a safari, or an exploration of one of the poles: difficult, physically exhausting, but educational and replete with possibilities for future anecdotes, should one survive.

Mr. Mulligan had joined them at the cocktail hour. He proved to be a pleasant, if slightly pompous man around forty. "So you've met our Mary Bradford," Mr. Mulligan had said, accepting a martini and settling down, with evident satisfaction, before the fire. "In that case I shan't have to describe her. I'm supposed to be a pleasant, if slightly pompous man around forty. So to my friends, but they always suspect I'm what the Scots call 'havering.' Do allow me to assure

37

you that while the last man to claim rectitude for himself, warranted or otherwise, I do not partake of orgies, alcoholic or sexual."

"I didn't know you were a writer," Kate said. "I thought you were a dreary academic, like me."

"Dreamy academics write, haven't you heard? In my case, I write far too many books entitled 'The Future of the Novel,' 'The Novel and Modern Chaos,' 'Form and Function in Modern Fiction'—to be properly alliterative that should have been in French Fiction, but alas, I don't read French. All my books talk about the decline of the old values and the emptiness of modern life—you get the picture. I suspect that none of them is any good, really, but I've published so many it was bound to be impressive after a while, and I have achieved not only tenure and a full professorship, but invitations to speak at women's clubs and even the possibility of running a sunrise semester on television next fall. What more can any man ask?"

"Who publishes your books?" Kate asked. "The University of Southern Montana Press?"

"No, oddly enough. The Calypso Press."

"Then you must be underestimating the books. If Sam Lingerwell's firm publishes them, they are no doubt first-rate."

"Do me a favor, kind lady, and rest content with that supposition. We may have to publish or perish, but I see no reason for perishing with boredom while we read what one another has published. The irrationalities of the academic world need not, after all, be pushed quite to their logical conclusions. Thank you, I should love another drink."

That had been at cocktails. Now, at dinner, Leo announced: "I got Mary Bradford right between the eyes this morning, I'm certain of it. Well, on the side of the head anyway, didn't I, William?"

"Very likely," William said, his major attention being on the chicken divan.

"It is really extraordinary," Emmet observed, "how we can't stop talking about that beastly woman. What did you 'get' her with, Leo? Something sufficiently deadly, I trust."

"Mary Bradford," Kate said, "is like a threat of war, or a strong suspicion that one is pregnant: it is literally impossible to think of anything else. But with sufficient control, one can at least attempt to converse on other topics. All the same, the woman does fascinate. She is so absolutely certain of her own rightness, and so absolutely, offensively wrong on every possible count. There I go again, you see. Leo, I'm not sure I altogether approve of your rifle practice, if that's what you are supposed to have gotten Mary Bradford with. Certainly I don't think you should talk about it."

"I haven't told anybody," Leo grumbled. "Nobody that counts."

"Just all the boys at the Araby Boys' Camp," Emmet said.

"They don't matter," Leo insisted.

"My dear Leo," Kate said, "you are as incurably urban as the rest of us. Each of those boys has a family simply longing to devour any available morsel of gossip. Last week, Reed, five miserable adolescent boys cracked up in a particularly nasty accident down the road; they must have been going eighty miles an hour, and the car was literally cut in half. Do you know, for two days the locals came from miles around to view the scene of the wreckage. The man whose property it was had to put up 'No Parking' signs, and only the summer people saw anything unusual in this behavior."

"I agree with you about the rifle all the same," Emmet said. "One is always reading about people being shot by accident with innocent rifles. I categorically deny the innocence of rifles."

"If a rifle has no bullets," William, who seemed to take this as a personal challenge, replied, "you might be able to kill someone by hitting him over the head with it, but you certainly can't shoot anyone. It's an excellent outlet for Leo."

"Shooting with an empty rifle?" Mr. Mulligan asked.

"It's got a telescopic lens," Leo hastened to explain,

before William could grab the ball and run with it. "I sight through the lens and learn to hold it steady when I pull the trigger. William's promised he will take me for rifle practice at the end of the summer. Of course, nothing happens when you pull the trigger, but sighting's fun. There's a man down at the farm who shoots woodchucks miles away, and never misses. Well, yards anyway," he added, catching Kate's eye.

"How can you be so certain there are no bullets about?" Reed asked.

"Oh, dear," Kate said. "We just found the gun in the barn; the gardener made sure it was quite empty, and I think he oiled it up a bit. Leo has most solemnly sworn *not* to touch a bullet with as much as a fingernail if he finds one, and I have looked pretty thoroughly and there really aren't any bullets around that I can see. Now you've immersed me in the midst of an awful qualm. But I don't really know very much about boys, and it does seem one is being spinsterish and antimasculine to refuse guns altogether; I have insisted that no one can, while under my roof, shoot a living thing, and that's probably ladylike enough."

"Why practice with a gun if you can't shoot anything, even in the distant future?" Mr. Mulligan asked.

"Well, Leo and William both assure me it will be rewarding to shoot at targets. I must say I don't approve of shooting at Mary Bradford, all the same. Impossible she no doubt is, as I am the first to admit, but ought you really, Leo, be aiming to kill even with an empty rifle? It does seem a bit in defiance of the spirit of the ruling, if not the letter."

"You're probably right," William said. "But I get up early with Leo" ("Damn early," Reed muttered) "and he likes to practice aiming in the mornings, and there, right before our eyes, simply begging to be aimed at, so to speak, was Mary Bradford. There she is, you know, every morning, yelling her head off."

"What on earth is she *doing* at five-thirty in the morning?" Reed asked. "Collecting dew-bespeckled toads?"

"Bringing in the cows to be milked."

"I do hope she doesn't see you aiming at her," Kate said. "Whatever Mary Bradford may be, we should maintain certain standards of decorum, should we not?"

"But she can't see us, Aunt Kate," Leo assured him. "In the first place, we're well hidden, what you might call ambushed. And then she doesn't expect to see anyone up at that hour, because all city slickers sleep till all hours she always says. And she makes so much *noise* yelling at those cows, you'd never believe. And some of the things she calls them. One morning . . ."

"Leo!" William's voice, together with a glance of the most ferocious aspect, caught Leo and transfixed him.

"My dear Leo," Emmet said. "Should Miss Fansler care to know what Mary Bradford says in the morning, she has recourse to the simple expedient of arising at that hour and listening. Meanwhile, I'm sure you will agree that to report in detail would be neither enlightening nor decorous."

"If she's that fascinating," Mr. Mulligan remarked, "I shall make a point of getting up to listen to her myself."

"Perhaps," Emmet said, "we ought to give a cow-catching party, coffee and vituperation, come in your nighties, and prepare to be shocked into a state of total wakefulness."

"Mr. Artifoni says," Leo remarked, "that shock is one of the most dangerous states following an accident. That's why it is so important to be careful, when there's been an accident, to . . ."

"Mr. Artifoni, I take it," Mr. Mulligan said, "is the local oracle in charge of the camp up the road."

"He is," Kate answered, "and there are moments when the convenience of having the A.B.C., as it is called, for Leo's sake, is distinctly overbalanced by the impact, not only of Mr. Artifoni's remarks, which are of course intelligent and helpful, if likely to apply to rather special situations"—Kate smiled at Leo—"but by the impact of seventy boys. Whenever I see a group of boys together I fear for the future of humanity. That no doubt proves why I am an old maid, and doing nothing about the future of humanity personally. Shall we have coffee in the living room?"

Reed was surprised but pleased to see Leo, Emmet and William disappear in one direction, while Kate led Mr. Mulligan and Reed himself back into the living room.

"Black, please," said Mr. Mulligan. "Say what you like about *my* orgies, Miss Fansler, and all you like about your own spinsterhood, I'm afraid if you continue to run so masculine and efficient a household, you are bound to be accused of having orgies yourself. Do you think," he asked, sipping the coffee with pleasure and accepting brandy, "we might join households and have an orgy, just to say we'd done it? Isn't one under some sort of obligation to offer grist to Mary Bradford's mill?"

"Exactly what I was thinking this afternoon," Reed said. "She positively bullies people into forcing her disdain. If I were her husband, which heaven forfend, I would shove my socks up her vacuum cleaner personally. What a nasty remark that sounds. Do you see what I mean?"

"Perfectly," Kate said. "You must get Emmet and William to join you in some suitably diabolical plan. But do please leave Leo and me out of it. Frankly, the woman terrifies me and horrifies me in equal proportions, and I *am* responsible for Leo."

"One doesn't, of course, care to sound in the least like our nosy neighbor," Mr. Mulligan remarked, "but might I ask, without appearing ghoulish, just who Emmet and William *are*? You do see, fair lady, that the very formation of the question anticipates an innocent and reasonable answer."

"You feel quite certain I am not going to tell you they are my lovers, my illegitimate children or my gang?"

"Quite so. I take it their duties revolve around Leo, who is your nephew."

"William's do. And Leo really is my nephew, by the way. No doubt it has already been suggested that

he is a small misstep I am passing off in this manner.
Is there, by the way, a word for auntly, counterpart to
avuncular?"

"I doubt it," Mr. Mulligan said. "Perhaps we can
invent one. I've always felt certain the major reason
Joyce wrote *Finnegans Wake* was to have the fun of
making up words. How about auntilary?"

"Not bad. Well, in my auntilary capacity I hired
William as buddy-cum-tutor to Leo: a companion, one
might say, for the young Telemachus. He, William,
happens to be a graduate student in the university
where I teach. One great difficulty in hiring male graduate students as summer companions for a nephew is
that, as Evelyn Waugh said, they like small boys either
too little or too much, but William is doing well with
Leo. Since Leo attends the A.B.C., William's duties
are not onerous; he has the use of this excellent library, his keep and the stimulating companionship of
Emmet."

"As well as a well-run house and the services of
your excellent Mrs. Monzoni."

"You know Mrs. Monzoni, Mr. Mulligan?"

"Not really. But I have heard tell, needless to say,
of that outrageous young woman, Miss Fansler, who
can't do her own cooking, cleaning or housework, or
even look after her own nephew. You are new to this
life, Miss Fansler. I have been summering here now
for nigh on a dozen summers, and I have learned
that the reason rural people imagine so much obscene
behavior is because they themselves, to a large extent,
indulge in it. Do you, by any chance, know the commonest crime on the police blotters of Vermont, to
pick a New England rural state?"

"Bootlegging?" Kate suggested.

"Perhaps," Mr. Mulligan said, turning to Reed, "Mr.
District Attorney can tell us."

"Incest, I imagine," Reed answered.

Mr. Mulligan nodded. "Father and daughter is the
commonest, though there are other forms."

"You horrify me."

"Naturally I do, dear lady. But if you stop and

think a minute, you'll see why the rural character, however sanctimonious his background, can imagine situations which we urban types consider within the grasp only of geniuses like Faulkner; your rural citizen is, so to speak, to the manner born."

"I'm certain Mary Bradford, whatever her iniquities, has never committed incest, nor had it committed in her family."

"You may be right. But I make some claims to being a judge of character, and there aren't all that many sins I would put past the ability of that lady, whose name I solemnly swear will not cross my lips again tonight, to perform. May I ask what Emmet is doing?"

"He's looking over Sam Lingerwell's papers and attempting to arrange them into some order which will make possible their ultimate disposal. Right now he's getting together the stuff on Joyce, and rather to my surprise, because Jane Austen is his idea of the only novelist worth mentioning, he's become very much interested, particularly in *Dubliners*. Emmet keeps muttering about Lingerwell's appreciation of Joyce's appreciation of the short-story form. Jane Austen, of course, did not write short stories. Did you know Mr. Lingerwell, since he was your publisher?"

"He had retired from active publishing before I came along. I heard he had bought this house, but I never saw him here."

"Well, Emmet is doing very well, all things considered. It's only this new excitement over Joyce's *Dubliners* that keeps him here, because he loathes the country, is terrified of snakes, shivers literally from head to foot at the thought of walking across an open field, and goes to the nearby town where we shop, population three thousand, for the sheer pleasure of walking on pavement and seeing a pigeon. He's very good for Leo too, even though Emmet's the sort who, if he feels like exercising, lies down till the feeling passes. But he talks to Leo as though they had both recently been members of the Jet Set and given it up out of boredom. It's a good experience for Leo, who has always been treated like a boy scout who had let down his troop."

"William and Emmet appear to be quite delightful counterparts," Reed said, "but do you think they are —perhaps 'wholesome' is the word I want—wholesome enough for Leo?"

"What wholesomeness they lack, Mr. Artifoni and his camp provide in ample doses; personally I find Emmet's effeteness considerably more wholesome than the robustness of the camp, but perhaps I ought not to admit it. Leo may begin the day here aiming idle rifles with William and discussing Joyce with Emmet, but he is then transported to camp, where, following the pledge of allegiance to the flag, and the Lord's Prayer, he learns the more abstruse aspects of the push shot, as developed by Bob Cousy."

"Kate," Reed said, "you are a remarkable woman. Bob Cousy indeed."

"My respects, dear lady," Mr. Mulligan said, rising, "and my farewells. This weekend I am having a cocktail party, and I would be delighted, Miss Fansler, if you and Mr. Amhearst, as well as Emmet and William, provided you can leave Leo with Mrs. Monzoni, will come by on Saturday afternoon. I hope I can promise you that nobody will so much as mention Mary Bradford."

Kate accepted the invitation for herself and promised to extend it to Emmet and William. Reed's response was a touch provisional. He did not know, he told Mulligan, from one moment to the next, whether he could stand the country any longer, not having, as Emmet did, the attractions of James Joyce. But should he be there . . .

"I am expecting two friends to arrive sometime tomorrow afternoon," Kate said. "You will be relieved to know that they are both female. Perhaps our household will quite overweight your party, should we all appear; on the other hand, I can certainly promise you that Grace Knole will add to any gathering."

"*The* Grace Knole. She *is* your colleague, isn't she?"

"No longer, alas. She has retired. But she is still very much *the* Grace Knole. She is coming with a young colleague of mine who is also a friend of William's."

"I shall be delighted to see all of you on Saturday, dear lady," Mr. Mulligan said, extending his hand with a ceremonious bow. "Until Saturday then, my special salutations to the illustrious Professor Knole. I am very pleased to have met you, Mr. Amhearst, and hope you choose to remain."

"Who *is* the illustrious Professor Knole?" Reed asked when Mr. Mulligan had bowed himself from the room. "Is she that illustrious?"

"In the academic world," Kate answered, "just about as illustrious as they come."

4

Grace

The illustrious Professor Grace Knole regarded, with a sense of loving desperation, the landscaped Taconic Parkway as it swept past her, or she along it, at seventy miles an hour. Eveline Chisana, who was driving the car, certainly knew her business; moreover, she, Grace Knole, was nearly seventy herself, like the miles per hour they were traveling, and ought not, rationally, to fear death. Eveline was not yet thirty and certainly demonstrated, so far, no suicidal tendencies. Old ladies should, if possible, not act like old ladies, particularly when they were outraged at being retired at the height of their powers. And damn good powers they were too, Grace thought, though I says it as shouldn't. "I suppose the car is in absolutely tip-top condition?" she asked, lightly, she hoped.

Lina, as everyone called her, grinned and slowed down to a decorous fifty-five. "Sorry," she said. "I expect I was thinking. Not a revolution over sixty miles an hour, I solemnly promise."

Grace stared at the young woman with interest. How different, she thought, from the young women of my day, who had, of course, to choose. Most young ladies today chose a house complete with husband and babies in suburbia, but even those like Lina who got Ph.D.'s and did brilliant scholarship, seemed to find time to drive, dance, cook and make love, all with equal expertise.

Line had not made love, not really, a fact of which she was thinking as the speedometer climbed high into the seventies; she had not really made love, nor, which was more to the point, had William. She planned to confront him, once and for all this weekend, across a constantly widening chasm of virginity. What a figure of speech! She could imagine her horror should it appear in a student paper. Chasms do not widen, she might write on such a student paper, at least not before one's eyes, to pick only the most obvious infelicity. Damn William. Damn. Damn. Damn.

"As a matter of fact," Grace said, "I shouldn't in the least mind walking. I *am* sorry to be such a nuisance, but I once had a misadventure in a Stanley Steamer, and you were going eighty. Perhaps it only looked like eighty from here."

Lina again slowed down, grinning her apologies. Dear Professor Knole. A frump, there was no other word for it, brilliant as she was. William said that the first time she entered the room to lecture, he thought the cleaning woman had taken leave of her senses and was about to make a speech. Until she opened her mouth, of course. A somewhat untidy, square person she was, with uneven hems dipping between calves and ankles, sensible walking shoes, hair which looked as though she had chopped it off herself with a paring knife. Yet at seventy she had turned down an offer of twenty-five thousand dollars to conduct one seminar on Chaucer, turned it down because she had other fish to fry. The right kind of frump to be, Lina thought. How much of life has she missed?

"From Kate's description," Grace said, "I gather her household is a rather unstable emulsion of small boys and James Joyce. I understand neither, of course, but I feel one should hold oneself open to new experi-

ences. I read *Lady Chatterley's Lover* recently when
it was legally reissued. It seemed to me that poor
Constance simply didn't have enough to occupy her
time."

"Should she have taken a course in medieval symbolism?" Lina mischievously asked.

"She might have done worse; in fact, in my opinion,
she did."

"There's no real connection between Joyce and
Lawrence," Lina said, amused. "Quite the contrary, in
fact. I understand they loathed each other's work."
Professor Knole might be the greatest living medieval
scholar, but to her all novels written since the industrial revolution were infantile distractions of which the
children, given sufficient time, would tire. "From what
William writes, Emmet has found some exciting letters
about *Dubliners*. William, of course, is very circumspect; his letters are always written with one eye on
the jury box."

"Which is *Dubliners?* That hasn't got Leopold
Bloom in it, has it?"

"No. That's just the point about *Dubliners*. The
stories are about different people in Dublin, all in
varying states of physical and spiritual paralysis." Lina
thought of the last story of *Dubliners*, "The Dead,"
of Gabriel Conroy's lust for his wife, and Michael
Furey, dead from standing in the rain, dead for love.
She thought of Bloom on Sandymount Beach in
Ulysses, dreaming of love, and the crippled girl, dreaming of love. Oh, God.

"I expect it only *looks* like eighty from here," Grace
said.

"Professor Knole," Lina asked. "Have you ever noticed how when you've something on your mind, you
seem always to engage in conversations about it, and
passages about it leap at you from books. It happens,
I think, with hungry men in prison camps and people
who've just given up smoking."

"And sex," Grace said, her eyes on the speedometer. "I used to notice that. Years ago, of course."

"We are nearly at the turning anyway," Lina said, slowing down.

Grace unfolded Kate's directions and began to read them aloud.

Despite the threatening rain, Reed and Kate walked across a field in which the hay had only just been cut. The brown dog, who gave every sign of having enlisted under Reed's banner, accompanied them. They walked on one edge of the fifty-acre field, and could see the baler drive in and begin to work on the other.

"He's got to gather it in," Kate said, "even though it probably isn't dry yet. If hay is rained on, after it's been cut and lying on the ground, it's finished. So much farm lore have I acquired." Together they regarded the baler as it scooped up the hay, transformed it, by some unseen process, into neat, rectangular bundles, and then shot the bundles into the wagon. "I never tire of watching it," Kate said.

"Let's cross the brook and climb the hill," Reed said. "I want to talk to you. I don't know why I should mind having my privacy invaded by distant machines, but I do. Shall we leap over this barbed-wire fence?"

"Of course not. You'll do something irreparable to your trousers. One lies humbly on the ground and rolls under. Thus." Kate accomplished the movement with a grace that bespoke practice. "One must be careful," she added, "to pick a place free of cow dung."

"Perhaps," Reed wistfully said, "if I had taken up tennis and kept leaping over tennis nets . . ."

"Vigorous people are so exhausting," Kate said. "This summer has been rather full of vigorous young people. All the young men who are counselors at Leo's camp, after they've finished eight long hours with the boys, begin to play heated games of basketball exactly when any sane person, it seems to me, would lie down with a cool drink. De gustibus, as they say."

"Kate?"

"Mmm."

"Will you marry me?"

Kate stared at Reed a moment, and then patted his shoulder. "That's very kind of you, Reed, it really is, but no thanks."

"I didn't ask you if you'd like to go out to tea. Good grief, I've heard proposals that one eat in a certain restaurant treated to more profound consideration."

"But there's probably an active choice between two restaurants. What William James called a forced option. I don't intend to marry."

"Meaning: there have been men you wanted to marry, and men who wanted to marry you, but they have never been the same men? Who said that?"

"Barrie. That's not what I mean, Reed. It's a matter of world enough and time."

"I didn't realize I was addressing my coy mistress."

"You know, never, until recently, have I stopped to consider what those words mean. The young lover says them, and we tend to think they mean only that life is short, youth but an instant, days fleeting. But it's more profound than that. Haven't you ever noticed how everyone you know has either world or time, but never both? People who have a world, a job, work, a place to put their lives—they are always short of time. It's the condition of having a world. But people with time: widows on park benches, old men, women with their children at school, even children at a loose end—these have time enough, but no world. Either world or time, never both. I've decided that I would rather have the world."

"And marriage, you are certain, provides only time."

"Time or, if you like, a different world for which I do not happen to be suited. This summer has been a revelation, Reed. I have experienced the world of domesticity for which I don't care, even with all the assistance provided by my brother, and I've also experienced time, unformed, filling the day. I think— well, I'll read a book, but then I think, really, I ought to work first, and then I don't get to work and in the end, like the ship-wrecked sailor in the poem by Milne, I shamefully lie about and do nothing at all."

"What happened to the sailor in the end?"

"All right, he got rescued. But I'm not shipwrecked, only momentarily becalmed. Reed, I am certain you don't realize what a selfish unwomanly, undomestic creature I am. I don't want to take care of anybody, really, or be the angel in the house. I'd rather ague about medieval symbolism with Grace Knole. Try explaining that in a woman's magazine."

"My dear, I don't want to be taken care of, and I can't say that your angelic qualities are the ones which, above all others, have overwhelmed me. Couldn't we share a world, and a certain amount of time?"

"The first thing you know, you'd want to have your boss to dinner, or he'd invite you to a party that couldn't be refused, and I'd find myself planning menus, and picking up a new evening dress because all your associates had seen the old one, and having my hair done, and making conversations with lawyers at dinner parties. As it is, we can be together now when the fancy takes us—and I prefer you that way, not hog-tied, hag-hidden. Just Reed; not *my* husband, *my* house, *my* drapes—rather two circles, as Rilke said, which touch each other. You know, you never told me, even that day on the hills, how England was."

"I had other things on my mind on the hills, as I have now. England was chiefly notable for the fact that you were not there."

William and Emmet emerged from the house and proceeded, with a certain amount of preparation, to occupy lounge chairs in the sun. Emmet applied suntan lotion, and William some idiotically named concoction which promised to, and astonishingly did, keep off insects.

"It may give you skin cancer," William cheerfully observed, "but it does prevent bites. Have some."

"Thank you, no. For some reason insects do not find me overwhelmingly attractive. In fact, they bite

me only in the absence of all other sentient life, and
then only as the final alternative to starvation. It's
supposed to have something to do with the nearness
of the blood to the surface of the skin. But there are
multitudinous theories."

"I shouldn't think you'd worry about sunburn, then."

"I don't *worry*," Emmet said. "Not brood, that is,
or tremble with anxiety. But I find it rather more sat-
isfactory to get evenly tan all over than to look as
though I'd been tipped in boiling water and had a
layer of skin removed, in flakes."

"It's none of my business . . ." William began.

"Always a sure sign that one is certain it is."

"You're probably right. Please omit the introductory
syllables. Why, then, do you affect these effete man-
nerisms, positively inviting everyone within earshot or
reach of gossip to consider you limp of wrist?"

"How do you know I'm not limp of wrist, as you
so coarsely put it—if you'll forgive my saying so."

"For one thing, you visibly restrain a shudder every
time you look at Leo."

"Oh dear, is it that obvious? I am sorry. I don't
mind some little boys, about five perhaps, with short
pants and Prince Charles haircuts, bless their well-
bred little hearts; Leo's a shade on the hearty side,
don't you find?"

"Leo's all right, as long as someone takes him seri-
ously, and treats him with dignity. You haven't answered my question."

"Which question, dear William, was that?"

"Oh, hell, Emmet, I admit you're entertaining, very
entertaining, and I particularly admire the way you
hold your liquor."

"Your own capacity is quite beyond praise."

"Not like yours. You simply get cleverer as the
evening progresses. Do you think your tolerance for
liquor is correlated with your nonattraction for mosquitoes?"

"It's not so much mosquitoes, Kate tells me, as deer
flies and a kind of flying ant. Whatever it is you're
obviously panting to say, why not *say* it?"

"I've nothing against fags, as it happens, though they do seem to have been swarming over the landscape recently, but you've been carrying on a passionate love affair for three years with a married woman. Why do you insist on suggesting that you couldn't be aroused to passion by anything more feminine than a choirboy?"

"May I respectfully inquire how . . ."

"Don't worry. It's far from common knowledge. Lina Chisana, who's coming up this weekend, went to school with your—ah—mistress. They're close friends. So are Lina and I. Neither of us gossips, as you can probably gather since your—ah—mistress told Lina. Let me, however, get this off my chest by admitting that I've told Kate. She, not unnaturally, was concerned about you and Leo. I've known *her* three years also, by the way, and she is reputed to be as sea-green incorruptible as Carlyle and as discreet as the tomb."

" 'Mistress,' " Emmet said, examining his legs for signs of sunburn, "has always seemed to me a word which might be used with more precision. Ought we not, etymologically, to reserve it for a woman financially supported by a man, usually maintained by him in some establishment, clothed by him, and expected to lie with him whenever he should choose to present himself?"

"I don't quite see . . ."

"Today we use the word for any woman to whom a man has made love. But, after all, why should she be his mistress? They are more properly one another's lovers, are they not?"

"Try telling that to Mary Bradford."

"Oh, screw Mary Bradford, if you can stand the idea. Which reminds me, since we're exchanging confidence in this charming, not to say girlish, fashion, how long is it since you, in your devout way, have had a woman, even in your dreams?"

William stood up. "I'm sorry, Emmet. Clearly, I've offended you. Please accept my apologies. I merely thought . . ."

"Oh, for Pete's sake, sit down. What so infuriates me about people committed to a life of chastity is that they seem to think its purity will be impugned if they discuss it. I wasn't trying to give you tit for tat, only to serve you, humbly, as you, I gathered, wished to serve me. Never mind. I'm damnably in love with a married woman who can't get a divorce, and who's married to a brute. The reason this summer's work is enticing me into a serious consideration of modern fiction is because I find the earlier, more melodramatic works a little too close to the bone."

"I'm sorry. Where is she this summer?"

"With her husband. Sailing about on a blasted yacht. Would you mind frightfully if we talked about something else?"

"All right; James Joyce. How does it go with the early letters?"

"I humbly thank you, well, well, well. Sam Linger-well was truly a great man. When the effects of your bug-away wear away, come in and let me show you a few letters. That is, if Leo and his athletic cohorts have not descended upon us. Do you know, I think I've met your Lina. Italian-looking, with an enormous vitality and an infatuation with eighteenth-century poetry. So she arrives with Grace Knole, does she? Imagine a household with three such distinguished and brilliant women in it, none of them married, and all existing in some emphatic attitude toward virginity."

"What in hell does that mean?"

"Elementary, my dear boy. One is now confirmed in her virginity, which only the grave is left to try. One is already regretting her virginity, which will soon, I would guess, be gladly sacrificed to the first man who presents himself in the right light amidst the properly alcoholic ambiance; and the third . . ."

"That's a goddamn offensive thing to say!" William stood up, upsetting the bottle of bug-away, which leaked onto the ground to the great distress of such ants as happened to find themselves in its path.

"And the third . . ."

"Emmet, for Christ's sake."

"Ah, I see that the vigorous Leo has returned, accompanied by Mr. Artifoni himself."

"Perhaps," William said, "I ought to apologize. I thought I meant well."

"No apologies in order, anywhere around, as far as I can see. Only a warning, or shall we say, a suggestion. I very much liked Miss Lina Chisana when I met her, and so does the woman I love. I hope you weren't offended by my evident assumption of Kate Fansler's nonvirginity; I'm sure she wouldn't be."

"Oh, damn virginity," William said.

"My point exactly," Emmet said, arising slowly and with dignity. "I quite look forward to the feminine injection into our household, particularly Grace Knole. What time are they expected, do you know?"

Mr. Mulligan, meanwhile, conferred with his cleaning woman-cum-cook about tomorrow's cocktail party. "It better not rain," he said, "because I've invited the whole town of Araby, and if we can't overflow on to the lawn, we shall have to overflow upward, toward the bedrooms. Offer up obeisance, Mrs. Pasquale, to whatever gods there be."

5

Araby

Whether due to the ineffectiveness of Mrs. Pasquale's prayers, or her gods, or merely to meteorological conditions, the weather on Saturday could scarcely have been worse. A steady downpour drenched the lawn and trees, leaving treacherous puddles on all the chairs and tables. "However," Mr. Mulligan remarked to Mrs. Pasquale, "one can never tell. They do, after all, say about Berkshire weather, if you don't like it, wait ten minutes. Have we dusted the bedrooms, Mrs. Pasquale?" Mrs. Pasquale, who was doing something with hard-boiled eggs, ignored him. He wandered off to stare from the living-room window.

The whole town of Araby was not, of course, coming—only the summer residents, and only such of these as were in their houses that weekend, and whom Mr. Mulligan found invitable. The year-round people would not be invited, nor expect to be. Mary Bradford, since her ancestors had apparently sustained some connection with the Mayflower, and her husband with Scarsdale, might have been invited on general social grounds, but her personality made such an invita-

tion better ungiven. It was tacitly assumed by the
summer people that the Bradfords could not attend
cocktail parties which were given inevitably, if not
consequently, at milking time.

The town of Araby, to quote from the standard
picture book on the Berkshires, is situated north of
Pittsfield, and owes its continuing rural character to
the fact that it was bypassed by the railroads. Certainly it is outstanding, if not unique, in western Massachusetts for being totally without any commercial
establishment whatever. Mail is delivered by Rural
Free Delivery, and Araby's inhabitants learn to live
with the fact that the nearest pack of cigarettes to be
bought is eight miles away. Taxes are high, since only
homes can be assessed to raise the money for roads
and schools. The summer people are taxed, in fact
though not in principle, at twice the rate of the year-
round people, which, since the summer people are all
clearly rich as Croesus, strikes the board of assessors
as only equitable. Mr. Mulligan had been known to
observe that his barn, a modest-sized building originally
designed to house horses, in which he now kept his
car, was assessed at nearly twice the value of the
Bradford barn, which contained a fortune in milking
equipment and hay elevators. But somehow the summer people never found the time or energy for a thorough investigation into these matters.

Araby's name was often commented upon, since almost alone among New England towns it was called
after neither an English dukedom nor an Indian
phrase. Tales of how this odd nomenclature originated
were widespread and of equal dubiety. The commonest of these relates how an early settler had fancied
himself a sheik, and liked to say he was "of Araby."
How he transferred this strange inclination into the
town's name was never properly explained, nor likely
to be.

By the second weekend in July nearly all the summer people were "up," and of these, nearly all
crowded into Mr. Mulligan's living room. The contingent from Kate's house, six strong, arrived halfway

through the proceedings, when the casual acquaintances were about to take their leave, and the hilarity was about to ascend to its highest decibel count. Mr. Mulligan greeted them with the greatest possible enthusiasm, and immediately announced that he intended to monopolize Grace Knole, because she was so distinguished and fascinating, and Lina, because she was fascinating and unknown to him.

"And the young man is well cared for, I trust," he called to Emmet and William as they helped themselves to martinis.

"Gone visiting," William said.

"A chum from that jolly day camp," Emmet said. "His turn to invite the chaps for wienies and marshmallows. What a round of social activity country living is, to be sure."

"Martini or scotch?" Reed asked Kate.

"What would you say if I asked for a Manhattan?"

"Whiskey and sweet vermouth? I'd know you'd changed so you'd probably consent to marry me, and I'd feel if you'd changed that much, I probably wouldn't want you after all."

"I've heard more gallant statements."

"I am not feeling gallant. Only old, foolish and oddly apprehensive."

"Of what, Reed? How unlike you. Whenever I get vague feelings of apprehension, you always accuse me of some particularly feminine idiocy."

"If you must know, our walks on the hills are the only part of this whole rural interlude I view with entire satisfaction. What was Mr. Artifoni, of the physical fitness and first-aid routine, going on about when we returned home from the hills yesterday?"

"Mary Bradford."

"That woman again? It seems scarcely believable."

"I couldn't agree more. It seems all the cars of parents delivering or calling for their offspring at the A.B.C. pass along our road, frighten Mary Bradford's chickens, and threaten her children, so she insists, with imminent extinction. She's taken to arriving at the camp, as it's dispersing and making loud, threatening remarks and talking of suing Mr. Artifoni. I believe she actually bullied a state trooper into giving speeding tickets to parents. Anyway, Mr. Artifoni has murder in his eye."

"So of course the first thing he did was to come around and talk to you."

"Well, I'm new around here, and therefore supposed to have a higher tolerance for local gossip and complaints. Also, he was delivering Leo home, which was nice of him. What are you eying, in your most district-attorney way?"

"Mr. Mulligan," Reed said. "He may not have orgies, but he's clearly the fastest worker since Don Giovanni, and with somewhat the same tastes, if I remember correctly the confidence of Leporello."

"I see," Kate said, "and so, blast him, has William. But after all, she's well up in her twenties, and supposedly knows what she's doing."

"I doubt very much," Reed said moodily, "if any of us knows that. Have another drink."

"I must say your glooming-about is scarcely flattering to me."

Reed looked at her. "The simple fact," he said, "is that I love you, and I wish you'd come back to New York and be properly sinful with me in an air-conditioned apartment. If you want my opinion, most city dwellers, one rung beneath the Jet Set and the writers of nasty articles for *Esquire,* are as innocent as a lamb unborn."

"Speaking of lambs," Kate said.

"I know, that's why the phrase came into my head, no doubt. Do you think he means to seduce her during the cocktail party, or immediately afterward, or will he first tell her all about Form and Function in French . . ."

"We had better go and talk to William."

"Emmet is talking to William."

"And clearly he's sunk twice, and is likely to go down a third time. Can you run interference?"

"Kate," Reed said, beginning to shoulder his way,

not too gently, through the crowd, "you must explain
to me about William."

"I can't explain William," Kate said. "I can't explain Emmet or Leo, or anybody. Emmet was explaining James Joyce to me this morning in agonizing
detail, and I've decided I can't explain him either.
William!" Kate called, having now edged within earshot.

William obediently swam the short distance toward
her through the currents of people.

"Where is Grace Knole?" Kate asked.

"Being told about artificial insemination by the
Osterhoffs."

"Ye gods, we had better go and rescue her. Would
you have any great objection to leaving now, if we
should be able to disentangle her from the details of
a cow's personal life?"

"Nothing could please me more," William said
fiercely, with a glance toward Mr. Mulligan and Lina,
"than to leave this instant."

"I find, don't you know," Emmet said, joing them,
"that my interest in artificial insemination is scarcely
breathless with fervency. And let's admit it, nonartificial insemination is much more interesting, and nonartificial, noninsemination is better still . . ."

"Oh, shut up," William ungraciously said.

"Though, of course," Emmet went on in a small
voice, bringing up the rear in their pilgrimage to Grace
Knole, "a nondiscussion of nonartificial noninsemination is best of all."

"Don't go," Mr. Mulligan said to Lina.

"But they're all leaving."

"Let them. I'll see you home. You can't desert me
now. I always tire of cocktail parties about this time,
and when they're your own you can't get up and
leave, the great inconvenience of giving cocktail parties as opposed to going to them. What are you drinking?"

"I think I had better stop drinking."

"Never stop drinking when you're still able to think

you had better stop drinking, the first rule of a successful life of indulgence. And of course a life of indulgence is the only possible life to be lived in summer houses in the country during the torrid months. Drinking is one of the few simple pleasures left in modern life, drinking and love."

"Is love really a simple pleasure?"

"To the complex, haven't you noticed? Norman Mailer has made a small fortune trying to transform love into a simple pleasure. But the only one who succeeds is James Bond, because he's so simple himself his pleasure can scarcely be otherwise. You puncture a girl's tires with a little gadget developed for 00 personnel, and then enjoy her in the grass dodging gunfire the while. The great mistake is unnecessarily to complicate life."

"I'm afraid I'm a rather complex person."

"Exactly. And as Oscar Wilde has told us, simple pleasures are the last refuge of the complex."

Kate and William walked home together. William having declared a frantic need for fresh air and Kate, downing all her civilized impulses. having decided to accompany him. Reed drove Grace Knole home, together with Emmet, whose eagerness to return to the Lingerwell papers was barely disguised. Kate had very mixed feelings about William, which were in no way simplified by the conviction that her determination not to interfere in his affairs was going, finally, to be overborne by the necessity of interfering in them. She ought not, of course, to have let Lina Chisana visit. But she had too late realized the intensity of the relationship between Lina and William. No doubt that relationship was such that only Henry James could have done it justice. Either William would have to let down the bars, or Lina, if she stuck with him, would have to dedicate herself to a life of placid friendships on the order of Grace Knole's, and between these two extremes Kate was hard put to decide which was the most unsatisfactory. Still, whether dalliance with Mr. Mulligan . . .

"What is that unspeakable blackguard's first name?" William asked. Kate dearly wanted to say "What blackguard?" but, never very good at sudden assumptions of naïveté, she merely said, "Padraic, spelled in transliterated Gaelic. I believe," she added, "he is known to his friends as Paddy."

"Where did he find his friends," William asked, "in the nearest seraglio?"

"The nearest seraglio is probably in Istanbul."

"I expect he's got one upstairs, the . . ."

"Now look here, William, I don't wish to sound middle-aged and assume any auntilary attitudes, but you have got to choose, you know, between a life of absolute celibacy and the love of a young woman. You simply can't have both, and the sooner you stop fooling yourself, the better."

"I know there are no standards left anywhere," William said, "but surely fornication is not yet the only way of life possible, even on the part of older women who are widely assumed to be models of virtue while seething with lust."

"All right," Kate said, standing quite still. "I myself admit a perhaps distasteful disinclination for either continence or matrimony, which doubtless makes me a criminal in your eyes. Don't interrupt. There *are,* however, crimes of omission, you know. If you spend hours and days and weeks with a young woman without even kissing her, you're asking for trouble and ought to take your lumps when trouble comes. I might add," Kate said, viciously kicking a stone from her path, "that since we are exchanging *ad hominem* remarks in this shameless fashion, let me suggest that if you want to be a priest, by all means go and be one. I'll give you all the support I can. But if you choose a life of noncelibacy, then try noncelibacing. Now, if you want to take the first train out of here, I'll try to find someone for Leo."

"There's a train from Pittsfield tomorrow morning. I'll call a taxi and take the train, since that seems to be what you wish."

"Oh, come off it, William, I wish nothing of the

sort. What would Leo do without you, particularly at five-thirty in the morning? Of course, I'd like you to stay."

"I can't have you thinking I meant to accuse you, I mean, it never occurred to me to suggest that you were . . ."

"A fornicator? Never mind. All relationships are changing, William, and rather to my surprise, for I have a great many old-fashioned tendencies, I think they're changing for the better. I still like courtesy, perhaps even formality of sorts. But I also think, as some pundit said, that the only crime sex can commit is to be joyless."

"I wish I could explain to you how I feel."

"Never mind. Concentrate on explaining the finer points of Hopkins' prosody, since that's the subject of your dissertation and you must, you know, get past your dissertation block. Remember, as C. S. Lewis so wisely said, it is easier to describe the threshold of divine revelation than the working of a pair of scissors."

Later that night, when Kate, having pleaded total exhaustion, had gone to bed with a stiff nightcap and fallen, not without much tossing and turning, into a troubled sleep, she was awakened by someone calling her name and knocking on her door. She thought at first that the house was on fire, and then that Leo had been kidnaped, these being the worries uppermost in her mind. But it was Lina, clearly on the verge of hysterics and prepared, Kate realized at a glance, to fly over the edge in the absolutely next moment. When Lina's sobs had subsided, however, and Kate had braced herself for another heart-to-heart with the younger generation about the perils of fornication on which she was prepared, with Lina, to take a decidedly spinsterish view, Lina sobbed out the name of Mary Bradford.

"Mary Bradford! What now, what possibly now?"

"She *said* she didn't think there was anyone home except just him. And naturally she leapt to the conclusion—there was a positive light in her eye, and nothing had happened, I mean, nothing really, but Padraic said he thought someone would probably slit the bitch's throat if she didn't watch out, so naturally, she won't waste any time spreading the story . . ."

"He said that *to* her?"

"Yes. When she walked into the house to see him, after the party. Kate, would you mind if I asked you about something?"

"Let's go down to the kitchen. I'm going to make some cocoa."

"Cocoa?"

"Why not? It's a soothing drink, isn't it? Now listen to me, Lina, I don't want to hear a lot of confessions you're going to loathe me in the morning for knowing. If Mary Bradford walked in before you met a fate worse than death, it may have been her best act in what has clearly been a misspent life. Padraic Mulligan isn't all that bad, even if I suspect him of not having a clue about either form or function in fiction of any nationality, but if you want to go off on a fling, I'm sure you could wait for a moment a little more spontaneous, if not affectionate. Coming down?"

"But," Lina said, when they were in the kitchen, "virginity can become a burden."

"Everything is a burden, especially nephews, students and the early letters of James Joyce. But remember, my dear, as Keats so wisely said, life is a vale of soul making. Do you know, I haven't the faintest clue how to go about making cocoa? Let's have a hot scotch sling."

6

The Dead

"Damn, blast and to bloody hell," Reed said. "Operator. *Operator*. We live in an age of automation, but Araby, of course, does not have dials. Moronic operators apparently hired from the nearest institution for retarded baboons. If I *knew* the number in Boston, my dear young woman, I would scarcely be troubling you. I *know* there are probably eighteen John Cunninghams in the Boston telephone book, we are simply going to have to try them all until we find the right one. Yes, it's Sunday, I do know the days of the week. No, I do not want to receive another call at this number, I want to find the right Mr. John Cunningham. Do you know," he said to Kate, covering the receiver with his hand, "I do believe I have gotten through to some functioning part of the child's brain."

"They're going to put dials in next year," Kate said.

"By next year," Reed said, hanging grimly on to the receiver, "I humbly trust that whatever happens in the town of Araby will be a matter of the most supreme indifference to all of us. Hello, hello, is this

Mr. John Cunningham? I am sorry to be bothering you so early, but did you by any chance attend Harvard Law School, class of '44? Believe me, sir, it is not my idea of a joke—an official of the electricians' union; I see. I'm sorry, but it is a matter of the greatest importance, I do assure you. Operator. *Operator.* On to the next John Cunningham, my child. From the list that Information has given us. The area code, like the city of Boston, remains unchanged."

"Reed," Kate said. "Couldn't you get his address from the Harvard Alumni Office, or some index of lawyers or something?"

"If they functioned on Sunday, no doubt I could. The police will be here in about five minutes, and we need a Massachusetts lawyer. Yes, Operator, well, let it ring. It was considerate of you," Reed said, turning to Kate, "since you were intent on opening a boardinghouse in the midst of rural iniquities, to open it in Massachusetts. As I went to Harvard Law School, I can at least draw upon some acquaintances and not throw myself on the mercies of just any lawyer. Very well, Operator, they have no doubt gone away for the weekend. Let's try the next John Cunningham. Kate, for God's sake, don't start crying. The woman isn't worth a tear, not a sigh. Miss Knole, take her off and see if you can talk some sense into her. Yes, Operator, I'm still here, though gladly would I be in city pent. Mr. Cunningham? Jack? Thank God. Reed Amhearst here. Fine, until an hour ago. Listen, do you happen to remember that night in Scollay Square when you said if there was ever anything you could do for me? Well, I hope when you said anything, you meant anything. I'm in Araby, and a woman has just been murdered. Araby. Near Tanglewood. Berkshire County. I think you'd better, if you don't mind. We'll arrange the details later. Good. If you can find Pittsfield, I'll tell you how to get here from there. By all means stop for a cup of coffee; I'm reasonably sure they can't arraign us for homicide in under four hours, particularly on a Sunday. Perhaps my being from the district attorney's office of New York will help some

—anyway, I'm certainly going to try it. Someone I cared for? That's the whole trouble, Jack, she was someone no one cared for. Righto. Hello, Operator. Thank you, my child, and bless you, we have come through." Reed hung up. "Come on, Emmet, let's see how our lady professors are doing."

It had seemed to Kate that someone was calling to her, and she was trying to answer the call, but William was marrying Lina and quarreling with Emmet over the ring, which Leo, dressed oddly in velvet doublet and hose, was insisting had to be used as a prize for push shots. Someone in the back of the church was calling. Her unconscious mind struggled vainly to incorporate this sound, which was threatening sleep, into her dream. Kate awoke, to find Grace Knole calling her name.

"What time is it?" Kate said.

"About six thirty, I think. Are you awake, or do you need time to pull yourself together?"

"What's happened? Leo? Lina and Mr. Mulligan . . ."

"Apparently one of the routine maneuvers in this household included rifle practice at five-thirty in the morning?"

"Has something happened to Leo?"

"Leo is fine, I think. But William has shot some woman who was fetching the cows. Some woman named Bradford. Shot her right through the head. I never did care for guns."

"There were no bullets in the gun. No one ever knew what kind of bullet went in the gun. Oh, my God. Is she dead? Are you sure?"

"I have seldom been as sure of anything. I took the trouble to go out and look at her, since everyone else seemed to be on the edge, if not in the midst, of hysteria."

"Is everyone up?"

"Everyone but Lina. Your Mr. Amhearst says we will have to call the police. Emmet wanted to go down and get her husband, but it was decided to wake you

first. I hope you can wake up fast enough to formulate
some plan, because except for Mr. Amhearst, who
says we have to have a Massachusetts lawyer, nobody
seems to have a clue what to do next."

"Emmet *had* better go tell the husband. No, I'll go.
It isn't really properly anyone else's job. It'll take me
one minute to get dressed."

But when Kate got downstairs she found Reed on
the telephone, and the others—all but Lina, who apparently was sleeping the sleep of the troubled young
—huddled about in the dining room, where the telephone was, looking, Kate could not help thinking
through her fears, like a group of stockholders meeting to dissolve a corporation. Leo was in the kitchen
receiving the ministrations of Mrs. Monzoni. When
Kate looked in, she had decided that, in the circumstances, Mrs. Monzoni was coping as well as anybody
else could, probably better.

Now Reed, finding Kate recovering over her second cup of coffee, turned to walk out the door.

"Where are you going?" Kate asked.

"To inform Mr. Bradford that his wife is dead. I
take it I shall find him in the barn, milking."

"Do you think," Emmet asked, "the cows made
their own way back, led by the thought of food, and
driven by the pressure of their swollen udders?"

"That's a point," Reed said. "Are the cows out there
now?"

"By no means," Grace said. "They weren't even
there when I went to look at her."

"I gather," Kate said, "from what Leo has told
me, that she never actually followed them all the way
home. They needed some urging from the rear, but
once started, they kept going. I think Bradford waits
for them in the barn, where each cow goes to her own
stanchion and is then locked in."

"Well," said Reed, "I'm on my way, so we will
soon know."

"I'm going with you," Kate said.

"You're staying here." Reed's eyes met hers. "If
Cunningham calls back, by any chance, or if the po-

lice arrive, tell them I'll return shortly. I think you'd better get Miss Chisana up, and make sure Mrs. Monzoni doesn't leave the house. Of course, no one is to touch the body or go outside."

"Well," Emmet said. "The sleuth at work."

When Kate returned from her errands Emmet was still talking. "William," he said, "hadn't you better say something—anything, really, just so I know you're quite all right: shocked of course, but basically sound. William!"

Kate walked up to William, who finally turned and looked at her. "Don't worry," he said, "I'm not hysterical. Just horrified and mystified in equal parts. It wasn't my fault. I didn't know there was a bullet in the gun; I didn't know there was a bullet in the house."

"William," Kate said, "who was shooting the gun, you or . . . ?"

"I was. I had taken it from Leo to sight through the telescopic lens, and I said, 'Here goes,' and pulled the trigger. I didn't think even with a telescopic lens I could hit anything. But of course I had the two lines crossed exactly at her temple. The trigger . . ."

"You could scarcely have missed at that distance," Grace said, "if you'd been cross-eyed and suffering from astigmatism into the bargain. I used to shoot," she said surprisingly, "when I was a girl in Montana. We didn't have telescopic lenses, of course, but I could have hit that woman at that distance in my shooting days with one good eye. Why were they shooting guns, Kate? This may seem an odd time to ask the question, but I didn't know about this morning target practice until just now."

"Now that the woman's dead," Kate said, "I can't imagine how I ever allowed such a thing. But when it was a boyish sport, it seemed somehow defensible. I remember defending it at dinner with Mr. Mulligan."

"So Mr. Mulligan knew about the target practice. Did anybody else?"

"Everybody," Emmet said. "Let's face it, Kate, there's nobody in the whole shining Araby valley who didn't know, and most of them probably wrote and told their friends and relations. Mr. Pasquale knew, I'm absolutely dead certain Leo told him, and Mrs. Monzoni, and all the boys at the camp and Mr. Artifoni and the counselors."

"Did Mr. Bradford know?" Grace asked.

"I'll jolly well bet he knew."

"Emmet!" said Kate. "Surely he would have said something."

"Said something? He probably jumped for joy and slipped a bullet in the gun himself."

"Emmet!"

"All right. And if either of you starts going *nil nisi bonum* etc., to me about that woman, I'll scream, I promise you. She was a scourge and a menace, and I can't see that her being dead means we have to lie to one another." Emmet bent down to pick up his red cat and held it to him, stroking it. "I'm not saying her husband shot her. Had I been her husband, I would have beaten her to death slowly with wet ropes. What I am saying is that William didn't really shoot her, and I think we should be determined that the police are going to know that."

"He shot her in fact," Reed said, coming into the room. "Kate, should we send Mrs. Monzoni down to help Bradford for a while?"

"How did he take it?" Grace asked, as Kate went off to the kitchen.

"He's stunned. He went right on milking his cows. Hello, there are the state police."

"Reed," said Kate, returning, "the police."

"All right, I'll talk to them. Now let's remember one thing. Ah, the sleeping Miss Chisana at last. Sit down, Miss Chisana, Kate will tell you all about it. For God's sake, tell the truth, all of you. Don't try to lie, or be heroic, or hide some idiocy because it sounds suspicious."

"Is William going to be charged with having shot her?" Kate asked.

"I'm not certain of the legalities in Massachusetts. He's certainly committed technical murder, probably in the third degree. But of course, as I believe I mentioned to you on another occasion, in another place, the police tend to regard the most obvious man with a certain interest."

"William had no reason to kill her," Lina said. "It isn't as though he'd shot me." William went over to stand beside her.

"O.K., everybody," Reed said. "Here we go."

"What have the police done so far?" John Cunningham asked. He was sitting at the table with Kate and Reed, gratefully consuming a large lunch. The others had gone upstairs except for William and Leo, who were shooting baskets outside.

"Not much," Reed said. "They haven't even removed the body, though they've covered it. The two state troopers who arrived can't have been, either of them, a day over twenty-four, and though I guess people had been accidentally shot before, it had never been a question of murder. They have notified the sheriff, and he or his representative will be along shortly, supposedly with photographers and a medical examiner, if that's what you call him in Massachusetts. It took all my persuasive powers to keep them from taking William away with them."

"I take it," Cunningham asked, "you've decided there's no point in maintaining it was an accidental death?"

"Someone accidentally dropped a bullet into a gun?"

"It's possible, you know. Every day of the week some kid loads a gun, or shoots one off accidentally. Perhaps someone was fooling around, heard someone coming, and left the gun loaded?"

"Who, for example?"

"What about the boy?" Cunningham asked.

"He swears he didn't load it, didn't even have a bullet for it or ever see one. I believe him, but I realize the sheriff might not," Kate said. "Frankly, however, I'd rather believe in murder than try to hang an accidental death on Leo."

"The gun was in the house always, except when those two morons were playing at target practice, is that right?" Cunningham asked.

"Yes."

"Had they had their target practice on Saturday morning?"

"Yes."

"Good. Then sometime during Saturday, or in the very early hours of Sunday, someone slipped a bullet into that gun. Someone who lived in the house is the most likely then."

"Not at all," Reed said. "We were all gone on Saturday afternoon. Anyone could have walked in. These country houses are never locked."

"It's really great," Cunningham said, helping himself to more strawberries. "Nobody can have an alibi, because we can't know when the bullet was put in, or for what time an alibi is needed. Nobody had to be within miles of the gun when it actually went off to have been the murderer. If I understand correctly your rather incoherent explanation of the prevailing situation, anyone, just about, from the families of the boys at that Araby Boys' Camp sanitarium right down to Miss Fansler herself, had ample opportunity and knowledge to put the bullet in the gun. Furthermore— These are delicious strawberries, by the way; grown locally, I assume. I am glad to discover that the natives do something besides laying nefarious plots for one another."

"I am happy to allow you your little joke," Reed said, "and able, with extraordinary broadmindedness, not to envy the disinterest with which you sit there guzzling strawberries and cream. However, I do object to having my explanation called incoherent. The household may be somewhat lacking in, shall we say, the ordinary components of normal domesticity, but my account of it was, I think, exact to the point of crystalline clarity, don't you agree, Kate?"

"I don't think this incident can be helping your

disposition," John Cunningham said, "or perhaps you've become sensitive over the years, sinking into pampered bachelorhood. Sensitivity is not allowed to us married men with four children, and swarms of in-laws who agree among themselves only in disapproving of the way we raise our progeny."

"Reed is the least sensitive, in a pejorative way, person I know," Kate said, with a vigor that surprised her. "Perhaps a practice of criminal law in Boston has accustomed you to the regular appearance of the bodies of neighbors, scattered about. You may not be aware of it, but I am in the delightful position of having either my nephew or his tutor arrested for murder or manslaughter, unless I or one of my guests is arrested instead. I am beginning to think the only solution, as Lord Peter Wimsey would have suggested, is poison for three in the library. In any case, I see no reason for berating poor Reed. He seems to me the only thoroughly sensible person in the whole dismal situation . . ."

"Who will, no doubt," Cunningham said, picking up her sentence and concluding it for her, "be able to prove that he is neither the murderer nor likely to perjure himself in defense of the murderer, should that person turn out to be a woman he loves or any member of her household. All right, sit down, both of you, and stop thinking you can behave like characters in a Henry James novel with the sheriff and very possibly the district attorney on his way. I am, as you point out, a criminal lawyer. I assume that that, together with an incident in Reed's and my past, is the reason you called on me at this juncture. Let us, therefore, try to see this whole situation as the police are going to see it, and not as we would like to have it represented in a beautifully wrought novel by a writer of exquisite sensibility. Keep quiet, both of you.

"Now." Cunningham pushed away, with evident reluctance, the bowl of strawberries. "Assuming that this murder was not the result of any long-seated grudge, and consummated at this moment by an extraordinary stroke of ill-luck because this household had at last provided the opportunity—and I need hardly add that we shall do everything in our power to prove that exactly that is the case—the murder must have been committed by one of a given number of people. To start with those nearest to the victim, her husband or, I should think from what you tell me of her, practically any other member of her family. Does she have any other family hereabouts?"

"Not that I know of," Kate said.

"Well," Cunningham went on, "it does sound as though we ought to call the woman's removal an act of sanitation and let it go at that. Still, a state that can blink at one murder, however desirable, will soon find itself blinking at thousands."

"If you believe that," Kate asked, "how can you be a criminal lawyer?"

"I don't blink at murder. I defend men accused of it. Isn't that rather a naïve question for a big, grown-up girl like you?"

"There is no need," Reed said, "to be offensive."

"Nor any intention, I assure you. Still, you're a district attorney, and when you find yourself with a body on your hands, you call a lawyer."

"I was thinking of our friendship in law school."

"Come off it, Amhearst. You two might as well accustom yourselves to a lot of straight talk, because that's what you're going to hear."

"My apologies," Reed said.

"And mine," Kate added. "Though my remark was, believe it or not, inspired more by curiosity than malice. No offense in the world."

"And none taken. Now. In addition to the husband, we have all the members of this household, each of whom loathed the victim, many for personal reasons, the others perhaps for personal reasons we are not aware of. I gather the delightful lady was not above a spot of moral blackmail, and in fact took particular pleasure in walking in on people in awkward situations, which reaches beyond this household to Miss Chisana and to Mr. Padraic Mulligan."

"You're not going to have to tell anybody that!"

Kate said. "You swore when we were frank about these things that—Look, I have betrayed a solemn trust because of the seriousness of the circumstances, but I did so only on the understanding . . ."

"Of the seriousness of the circumstances. There you go again, all purity and righteous indignation. Remember, the police are going to find out a good deal, and we have got to know more. Whether or not we use our information is a decision which can and must wait for a later time. It's no good sweeping dirt under the carpet, if the first thing the police are going to do is lift up the carpet and inspect the floor beneath it with a microscope. What was I talking about?"

"Mr. Mulligan?"

"Ah yes, and Miss Chisana. Then we have Mr. Artifoni, according to my list, he of the A.B.C., who appears to have a pretty motive . . ."

"Hardly a motive for murder."

"Perhaps a motive for a murder that was supposed to be, for all intents and purposes, undetectable. Then there are the Pasquales, of whom Mr. works in your garden, and Mrs. works for Mr. Mulligan. Then there is Mrs. Monzoni, whose loathing of the victim was expressed to every possible person on every possible occasion. These named, we have remaining, apart from person or persons unknown to us, only the members of this, you must pardon me, my dear lady, eccentric establishment. A small boy; his tutor, who seems vowed to a life of celibacy while passionately in love, and suffering from a block in his dissertation. Another doctoral candidate, acting as scholar and researcher, who seems to combine the manner of Oscar Wilde with the sex life of Frank Harris. He is in need of a shot in the arm, academically speaking, and who knows—do you, dear lady?—what he may have found among the late Mr. Lingerwell's papers—all right, make a note and tell me later. Then we have the two female guests—Lina Chisana, apparently a brilliant young woman of enormous vitality and charm, temporarily encumbered with the weighty burden of virginity, and Professor Grace Knole . . ."

"She is completely without either motive or opportunity."

"And therefore deserving of special attention."

"She is seventy and extremely illustrious with no conceivable . . ."

"No doubt you are right. At the same time I could enlighten you with tales of seventy-year-olds of illustrious reputation who went beautifully off the rails in a last, desperate bid for power or experience."

"Surely," Reed said, "that occurs somewhat earlier in life."

"In most cases. Exceptions, while statistically small, may be numerically staggering. To these we add you two, but let's for the moment assume your innocence established. After all, you're hiring me."

"Yes," Kate said, "about your fee."

John Cunningham waved a dismissive hand. "Don't worry about that now," he said grandly. "We have more important things to discuss. Besides," he added, "I stopped long enough this morning in my pursuit of relevant information to determine that you are related to the Wall Street Fanslers, half a dozen of whom are, I understand, your brothers."

"Cunningham," Reed said, "I hope it is clearly understood that any debts to be incurred by this investigation or defense . . ."

"Reed," Kate said. "This is my eccentric establishment, as Mr. Cunningham calls it, and it was my maniacal permission which allowed the gun to be shot off, neither of which did you approve of for a single instant. You included, if memory serves, the entire rural ambiance of your condemnation. So I will not have you assuming any financial responsibility . . ."

"Ladies and gentlemen." Mr. Cunningham stood up. "Perhaps my joking is on the heavy-handed side, though if you get an idea that I'm a crude bastard, we will get along in this investigation rather faster. Let's talk about fees when we know if there's any case here at all, and whether this will ever go to court. In the event that either of you turns out to have murdered the loathsome lady in a fit of misspent passion, I shall gracefully retire from the scene, and you can call in Louis Nizer. Ah, a car. The gentlemen, I doubt me not, from the Commonwealth of Massachusetts, Berkshire County, or do you think they've called in an assist from the Boston Police Department? Now, let me do the talking at first, except when a question is asked directly of you, and answer then as simply as possible. Remember, the abilities of the police to appreciate the complexities of a novel by Henry James, or even Jane Austen, if it comes to that, are considerably less than mine, and I suppose you've gathered by now that mine would hardly win me a bachelor's degree from a backward agricultural college."

Reed, coming up to stand behind Kate, put his hands on her shoulders as John Cunningham went forward to greet the authorities.

7

Two Gallants

The two men who entered seemed courteous enough. Kate realized, a bit guiltily, that she had built them up in her mind as ogres. John Cunningham stepped forward to introduce himself and, having introduced Reed as an assistant district attorney of New York County, indicated his own position as counselor to Miss Fansler. The two Berkshire County officials, while greeting with definite cordiality a professional peer, seemed to Kate's perhaps oversensitized perceptions, to fear his allowing their camaraderie to lead to unorthodox, unwelcome familiarities. But Reed continued to efface himself, to their relief, and they addressed their questions, mostly to Cunningham, but partly to the room at large. Kate had the impression that should she insist on speaking for herself, she would meet with distinct, if veiled encouragement.

"Your colleagues, I gather," John Cunningham said, walking to the window, "are proceeding with their accustomed rituals out of doors. They have located the body?"

"Yes, thank you. They'll be busy for quite a while

outside. Then, with your permission, they will come inside. Might I ask to see the murder weapon and the young man who fired it named"—here he consulted a note—"William Lenehan? The men can then get started with the ballistic and fingerprint problems."

Cunningham turned questioningly to Kate. "The gun is on the back porch," she said. "I'm certain it will be fraught with fingerprints, if that's the right phrase. William is outside playing basketball with Leo. About Leo . . ."

"I'm certain," John Cunningham interceded, "that we need have no fears about Leo. The gentlemen here will talk to Leo, a minor, only in your presence, and with your permission. Perhaps he ought to come in so as not to witness the removal of the body."

One of the men, at a nod from the other, disappeared to direct the fingerprinting of William and the gun, and the return indoors of Leo. He reappeared shortly.

"Who exactly is the owner of this house?" the first man, who in his companion's absence had reminded Kate that his name was Stratton, inquired. He had the air of one who begins with simple matters.

"Miss Fansler," Cunningham suddenly said. "Who does own this house?"

"Miss, or perhaps Sister, or would it be Mother, Lingerwell."

"I beg your pardon," Mr. Stratton said.

"She means a religious, no doubt," his companion added.

"Ah, of course; and how is she related to you?"

"Perhaps," Kate said, "we could sit down. Might I offer you something to eat or drink? Mr. Cunningham found the strawberries exceedingly . . ."

"No thank you," Mr. Stratton said. "Let's sit down by all means. Go on, Miss Fansler."

"Miss Lingerwell—perhaps I might just call her that —is no relation to me at all. In fact, I don't know her very well anymore."

"Then she is merely the landlord, from whom you are renting the house?"

"Well, you see," Kate said, feeling like a doubtful swimmer who has just leapt into the midst of a very deep, very cold, quarry pool, "I'm not renting the house. Could we, Mr. Cunningham, begin at the beginning?"

"And where is the beginning, my dear woman?" Cunningham asked. "With Adam and Eve, or the discovery of America, or the settlement of New England, or the founding of the town of Araby . . ."

"Mr. Cunningham." Mr. Stratton's voice indicated that he was coming to grips with fundamental matters. "Am I to understand that the members of this household have been instructed by you to answer questions only in your presence, and with your permission?"

"That is within the letter and meaning of the law, is it not?"

"Certainly. On the other hand . . ."

"On the other hand, I quite see your point of view. You would rather pursue your investigations undeterred by me. Well, proceed, my two gallants. I shall return to Boston and to my own affairs, from which this unfortunate occurrence diverted me. Perhaps you will be good enough to indicate whether you intend to take legal action against William Lenehan."

"He will be arraigned, certainly and then, in all probability, released in the custody of—you if you should choose, Mr. Cunningham."

"Not however today, I gather."

"I think not. Tomorrow."

"Very good. I shall return or, more likely, meet you in the courthouse. Good-bye, Miss Fansler, for now. Thank you for those truly excellent strawberries. Reed, might I have a word with you on my way out?" Kate watched him go, accompanied by Reed, and began to feel, for the first time that day, a rising sense of panic.

"You were telling me, Miss Fansler, that you do not rent this house?"

"Perhaps I do rent it technically. I don't know. I'm here trying to bring some order into the papers of the late Samuel Lingerwell. Mr. Emmet Crawford is helping me."

"Mr. Crawford is no relation to you."

"No. He is a graduate student in the university where I teach."

"I see. And Mr. Lenehan's duties are in connection with the boy? Is that correct?"

"Yes."

"Is Mr. Lenehan any relation to you?"

"No. He is a graduate student also. I am really afraid, Mr. Stratton, that I have an unfortunate talent for unconventional situations. I can never decide whether odd things happen to me or, as Shaw suggested about himself, I happen to them. I fear you must find all this dreadfully strange."

"Then apart from the boy, who is your nephew, no one in the household is related to you at all, or even very well known to you?"

"I cannot think," Kate, who had been priding herself on the remarkable degree of calm she was maintaining, burst out, "why the matter of relationships is one which strikes you as of such overwhelming importance. True, I am not living in the bosom of my family. However, since my parents are dead, my family is, so to speak, without a bosom—though I have to admit I should not have the slightest desire to throw myself on it, should one be discoverable. I can quite see that from the police point of view, this household must appear a dreadful strain on your descriptive powers, but perhaps if you look at it in the light of a summer study group, complete with casual nephew, it will appear a more orderly phenomenon."

"Is Mr. Reed Amhearst any relation?"

"I shall go mad, round the bend, completely and absolutely crackers. Reed Amhearst, if you must know, Mr. Stratton, is a man with whom I happen to be . . ."

"Spending what was supposed to be a quiet weekend," Reed said, walking into the room. "You've no objection to my listening in, silently, have you, Mr. Stratton?"

"Perhaps," Mr. Stratton said, in a voice which admitted no possibility of irritation, "I can conclude my questions on this household. Present here also are, according to my notes, a Miss Eveline Chisana, and a Miss Grace Knole, as well as . . ."

"Both ladies should be referred to as Professor," Kate said, with some asperity. Reed might have saved her from God knew what ghastly admission, but she was not about to let Mr. Stratton get away with anything. She had taken quite a dislike to Mr. Stratton, who appeared, insofar as one could perceive anything through his bland manner, to be returning the sentiment in spades.

"Professors of what?"

"English and comparative literature. Professor Knole is a specialist in medieval literature, Professor Chisana in the eighteenth century."

" 'Be not the first by whom the new is tried/ Nor yet the last to lay the old aside,' " Mr. Stratton surprisingly said.

"Exactly," Kate agreed.

"And what are you a specialist in, Miss Fansler?"

"Victorian literature. 'Ring out, wild bells.' 'Oh, love, let us be true to one another.' "

"I prefer the eighteenth century. Order."

"Professor Chisana's views exactly. I'm sure you'll get on very well."

"She and Professor Knole are guests here?"

"Yes."

"Were they previously acquainted with any members of the household besides yourself?"

"Professor Chisana is a friend of Mr. Lenehan's. Professor Knole may, before her retirement, have known both of them—I'm not certain. She certainly knew Emmet Crawford, since she recommended him to me. She was head of the department in which both men are graduate students."

"Mr. Amhearst and the boy are also your guests?"

"Yes. Though Leo might be called a member of the household."

"In what exactly do Mr. Lenehan's duties consist?"

"He offers companionship and instruction to Leo. Leo had fallen rather behind in his schoolwork. Under William's direction, Leo writes essays, does problems in arithmetic, and learns to relate coherently his experiences, at camp and elsewhere." Mr. Stratton looked as though he thought Kate too could profit from lessons in relating her experiences coherently.

"I wonder," he said, "if you would have any objection to my questioning the other members of your household? I believe we have determined who all of them are, except for the help, indoors and out."

"Whether they talk to you seems to be their decision, or the law's, not mine."

"Very well. And is there a room in which I might question them quietly."

"There's the library, where Emmet works."

"That will do very nicely, thank you. Only one more question, Miss Fansler, for now. How well did you know the dead woman?"

"Not very well. On the other hand, I'm not sure there was much to know. As you will no doubt gather if you pursue your investigations, she was not widely loved."

"Had you any reason to dislike her?"

"Apart from the fact that she had all the endearing characteristics of a bobcat, no. Whom do you wish to see first?"

"Since Mr. Crawford is supposedly in the library, we might as well start with him." They all stood up. "I hope, Mr. Amhearst," Mr. Stratton said, "that you will not mind answering a few questions later on."

"Certainly not. Might I, at the moment, usurp the privilege of making a suggestion? After you have questioned everyone in this house, you might turn your attention to the rural community outside. I strongly suspect that you'll find the cause of your crime there. Mary Bradford was hated by many, and it seems to me likely that this household, with its lack of surface conventionalities, appeared a likely agent for the carrying out of the murderer's plans."

"We have every intention, Mr. Amhearst, of pursuing that line of inquiry. Will you be kind enough, Miss Fansler, to show us to the library?"

"What's the other fellow for?" Kate asked Reed, as they walked out onto the lawn. " 'I have a little shadow that goes in and out with me,/And what can be the use of him is more than I can see;/He's just exactly like me from my toes up to my head . . .' I hope the rest of it isn't appropriate. Do you really think the answer is in the rural community outside, as you so stuffily put it?"

"The other fellow—to take your questions in the order in which they were presented—is notetaker and witness, should one be required."

"And protector of Mr. Stratton, should any of us go beserk and try throttling the pompous son of a . . ."

"Kate, he's only doing his job, though I do admit his manner is a trifle unrelaxed."

"Unrelaxed! He makes a stuffed shirt look like a crumpled nightgown. It occurs to me, not for the first time, that you are something special in the way of a district attorney: you're neither familiar nor pompous with people you meet, and that's not only commendable, it's extraordinary."

"To answer your second question . . ."

"I take it back; perhaps you're pompous after all."

"I don't know if the crime is really outside this household. I'm reserving judgment, but I thought it well to direct Mr. Stratton's attention in that direction. Kate, will you please behave yourself? You were allowing him to annoy you into admissions you would not ordinarily make, and that is exactly his intention. Whatever were you about to say when I came in?"

"None of your business. If you wanted to find out, you should have stayed outside and listened. Reed, you're not really worried that I'm going to land us in some frightful situation by letting my tongue run away with me? I've nothing to hide, really, and you yourself said we weren't to withhold . . ."

"Do you know why I want to marry you? Because if it's not exactly legal to beat your wife, it's less illegal than to beat a woman to whom you're not related in any way. Shall we get married?"

"You just want to marry me so I can't testify against you in court. You're afraid I'm going to tell Mr. Stratton that you wanted to marry Mary Bradford in order to stuff your socks up her vacuum cleaner. Reed, Reed, where is this going to end?"

"Do you know, I'm frightfully worried about where it's going to end, and I think, far from being a mare's nest, this whole situation may well be a hornets' nest about to explode. But though I'm certain I ought to be lecturing you about the proprieties, and brooding about what all those innocents are saying in there, and feeling mournful over the death of Mary Bradford, who met, God help her, a mean and violent death, I'm aware of only one desire . . ."

"Which had better, according to your own precepts, be unexpressed. Do you know, you're beginning to talk like me, full of subordinate clauses, and penultimate climaxes, interspersed with periodic sentences. We can't possibly disappear, can we?"

"Not possibly."

"Why did Cunningham disappear? Do you think he's given us up as a bad job, or were we taking too much of his time?"

"He felt that for all of us to talk only in the presence of a lawyer would not give the tone of innocence it is so important to convey. Cunningham's clever as hell, and he knows the police know it. If he walks off leaving us to their tender mercies, it's as good as saying he doesn't even think they've got a case."

"Doesn't he?"

"All Cunningham's clients are innocent by definition, didn't he tell you?"

"I hope we are innocent. But if we don't find the murderer, and I don't see, really, how we can, won't it be a dreadful cloud hanging over us all?"

"Oddly enough, I don't believe the innocent need fear the clouds, not in this case. Hello, speaking of innocents, we appear to be about to entertain Mr. Milligan."

"The news must be all over the valley. You see before you a man making straight for the horse's mouth."

"Ah, Miss Fansler," Mr. Mulligan said, approaching. "What sad news."

"You refer to the death of Mary Bradford?"

"Death is always sad. But I referred, actually, to the inconvenience to your household. Might I offer any assistance?"

"Come in and have some lunch. If the police should join us, you can help me to behave myself in their austere presence. If not, we can exchange gossip. Had any orgies lately?"

"Kate," Reed said between his teeth, "I have definitely decided not to wait for marriage. I tell you what, Mr. Mulligan," he said, raising his voice to its normal range, "perhaps Miss Fansler will allow us a little sherry before lunch, since the circumstances are, shall we say, a bit exceptional."

Kate stuck out her tongue at him.

8

Ivy Day in the
Committee Room

By four o'clock Mr. Stratton had finally worked his way through the household, including the cook and gardener. Mr. Pasquale, indeed, was never there on Sunday, but aware of the presence of the police, he had arrived and begun weeding an already weeded flower bed, making it manifest that he hadn't the smallest intention of leaving until the fall of night or the departure of the police, whichever should occur first. The news of Mary Bradford's gruesome death had spread far and wide, beyond the bounds of Araby, and the sightseers were already beginning to converge. The police were coping with these, but Kate was heard to mutter that they had better get some 'No Parking' signs, as in the case of the automobile accident, to which Reed answered that there were always, in any community, rural or urban, people to whom a murder was an experience invigorating in the extreme, and the scene of a murder fascinating beyond description. He supposed these were the sort who attended hangings in the eighteenth century, and drawing and quarterings in Tudor times.

Mr. Stratton consented, since it was four o'clock, to partake together with his cohort, of a sandwich and a glass of milk. He consented reluctantly, overborne apparently by the obvious hunger pangs of his associate and the information that the nearest restaurant was sixteen miles away, coming and going. Following this repast, he requested to see the three "lady professors" in the library. Food had clearly not improved his disposition, which had in addition been tried to the uttermost by his attempts to grapple with James Joyce.

"Perhaps," he said when they had all forgathered, "you three, since you are all professors of literature, can explain James Joyce to me."

"I am reminded, Mr. Stratton," Grace Knole said, "of a novel by Thomas Hardy, a minor novel I believe, though the name escapes me. In this particular work, a man, courting a young woman, is forced to admit to her that he has also proposed in the past to her mother and grandmother."

Mr. Stratton looked as though he was already regretting his decision to consult them. "But how," he began, "could one man . . ."

"I suggest that you not get bogged down in the mathematics of it now," Grace said. "Turn it over in your mind when you're trying to get to sleep tonight, remembering that women in those days married and had children at sixteen, and a good thing too, you are doubtless thinking, forced into confabulation with three spinsters of varying ages." The look on Mr. Stratton's face indicated that that was exactly what he had been thinking or, to be more exact, had been about to think, for Grace Knole's mind, working more rapidly than that of any other brilliant scholar, was bound to be several steps ahead of a mere policeman's.

"About James Joyce," Mr. Stratton said.

The three looked inquiringly at him.

"There's a story here, now, called 'Ivy Day in the Committee Room.' While eating the lunch Miss Fansler was kind enough to offer me, I read that story in a book Mr. Emmet Crawford in his turn was kind enough to offer me. I had asked him, since he seemed to keep mentioning this writer James Joyce, if there was anything short of his that I might read. The story was eighteen pages long, and I didn't understand a word of it. Neither," he added, "did my associate."

"Yes," Kate said. "It's always been a difficult story, as a matter of fact. Do you mean, Mr. Stratton, that nothing seems to happen in it?"

"That's exactly what I mean."

"But that, you see, is the whole point. Nothing is happening in Ireland at all. All the people are dead, actually; incapable of love."

"Like Mary Bradford," Lina said.

"Now that you mention it," Kate said, "exactly like Mary Bradford."

"Is that," Grace asked, "why Forster said of Joyce that he was throwing mud on the universe?"

"Forster was speaking of *Ulysses,* and in any case I think he's retracted the statement since. He said that when everyone thought of Joyce as immoral."

"There's a story I heard," Grace said, "of someone's dining with Joyce, and raising a glass of wine with a toast to immorality. 'I won't drink to that,' Joyce is supposed to have said, turning down his wineglass."

"It was white wine," Kate said.

"Does it matter," Mr. Stratton asked, in tones of one who has suffered long and silently, "what color the wine was?"

"Of course it matters," Kate said. "That's the whole point about Joyce's work. In 'Ivy Day in the Committee Room' the most important thing that happens is a bottle goes 'Pop.' "

Mr. Stratton looked as though he would soon go "Pop" himself.

"What's Ivy Day, to begin with?" he asked.

"There's a book, paperback, I believe, called *A Reader's Guide to James Joyce,*" Grace said, "by William York Tindall. You must allow me to present you with a copy. I get a faculty discount, a privilege extended even to emeritus professors. Tindall says, if I remember correctly, that everything in the story acquires meaning by reference to Parnell. Do I understand you to be suggesting, Mr. Stratton, that everything in this case acquires meaning by reference to James Joyce?"

"Is Ivy Day Parnell's birthday then?"

"That's funny," Kate said. "I'm not certain if it's his birthday, or the day he died, or something to do with the divorce. But on that day, October 6, everyone in Dublin who wishes to bask in remembrance of Parnell wears ivy in his buttonhole. They are all paralyzed of course."

"Of course," said Mr. Stratton.

"Why do you supose Emmet showed Mr. Stratton 'Ivy Day in the Committee Room'?" Lina asked.

"It was Joyce's favorite story," Kate said. "Everyone else's favorite, of course, is 'The Dead,' one of the great stories in the English language."

"What's that about?" Mr. Stratton asked.

"About a man named Gabriel Conroy who has never learned to love," Kate said. "About the truth that everyone in Ireland is dead, except perhaps the dead."

"Cheerful sort of chap he sounds," Mr. Stratton's associate surprisingly put in.

"*Ulysses* is more cheerful," Kate said.

"Isn't that supposed to be an immoral book?" Mr. Stratton asked.

"Neither legally nor actually," Kate said. "In point of fact, it's one of the most moral books in the language. Bloom is bringer of love to a dead city, and to a not-yet-artist who has not yet learned to love. Light to the gentiles."

"I thought there was a lot of sex in it," Mr. Stratton bravely said.

"There's a lot of sex in life," Kate answered.

"In some lives," Grace Knole said. Kate avoided Lina's eyes.

"Would you say," Mr. Stratton asked, "that Joyce is important?"

"Of course he's important," Grace said. "Read

Richard Ellmann's biography. Brilliant. Not, I believe, in paperback. Too expensive for me to offer you a copy, even with a faculty discount. Perhaps," she suggested, "you could put it on your expense account."

"I never know what people mean by important," Lina said.

"All these letters of his lying around here," Mr. Stratton said, before a literary argument could ensue. "Mr. Crawford tells me the Library of Congress and lots of universities have been after them."

"Ah," said Grace Knole.

"Odd that a woman should be killed at a house with a collection of letters from an Irishman."

"There was probably no connection at all. Now Mary Bradford was the sort," Kate added, "who would have found *Ulysses* a dirty book, and Bloom a dirty man. Of course," she added, "Joyce didn't have much use for WASPS."

"Wasps?" Mr. Stratton asked, with the air of one prepared to hear anything.

"White Anglo-Saxon Protestant; Puritan; Calvinist."

"I'm a Calvinist," Grace Knole said.

"I am sure he would have made exceptions." Kate smiled. "In fact, we know he did. But his vision encompassed mainly the world of Catholics and Jews. There was a time, you know, when he thought of being a priest. 'I have given up the Society of Jesus for the society of Jewses,' he's supposed to have said."

Mr. Stratton and his associate looked rather shocked. "You seem to know a great deal about Joyce, Miss Fansler," Mr. Stratton said.

"Very little, I assure you."

"I thought you said your specialty was Victorian."

"So it is, but we are not all allowed to stay sheltered and unmolested within our periods, however vast. I give a course in the history of the English novel, under which title we include the Irish."

"Well," said Mr. Stratton, rising, "I think I had better speak to Mr. Mulligan now. I understand he was here. Is he still, do you know?"

"Talking to Emmet, I believe," Kate said, rising also. "Shall I send him in?"

"If you would be so kind," Mr. Stratton said. "Thank you for your literary help, all of you."

"*Our* pleasure," Grace Knole said, leading the way from the room. "But what," she asked when the door had shut behind them, "is the name of that other man, the one who's always with Stratton but barely utters?"

"I haven't a clue," Kate said, "but I call him M'Intosh."

"Why?" Lina asked.

"Read *Ulysses*," Kate maddeningly said.

"I shall make a note of it," Grace said, "and of all the other interesting information just received. *White* wine." She took a notebook from her pocket and wrote in it.

"Do you make a note of everything?" Lina asked in amazement. "Is that how you remember everything?"

"Absolutely. Even the frightful things."

"I have no trouble remembering them," Lina laughed.

"Oh, yes you do. When Alice picks the Red King out of the grate he says, 'I shall never forget the horror of that moment,' and the Red Queen says, 'You will, though, unless you make a memorandum of it.' Since," Grace went on, returning the notebook to her pocket, "we have been ushered from the committee room, shall we take a walk? I wonder if it is milking time, by any chance."

"They're probably just finishing up," Kate said, "to go by what Leo has told me. But of course I did *not* make a memorandum of it."

"Do you think Mr. Bradford would mind our intruding on him, especially today?"

"He's rather patient about it, actually. It seems to me Leo and William used to spend every afternoon down there at milking time, till they knew more about it than he did. Anyway, maybe we ought to be detectives and see how he's reacting. Shall we go? Across the fields, or down the road?"

"The road, I think," Grace said. "I understand how

to cope with cars better than those dangers I know not of. With which, incidentally, the rural life seems to be replete. I have known many raging passions in my time, from naked ambition to naked lust, but no one has ended shooting anyone else, though a few to be sure have ended their own lives. I blame it not on the greater inherent violence of rural life, but on the greater familiarity with guns and violent death. I expect after you have many times seen a deer or wood-chuck blown to bits, the thought of a human being blown to bits is that much less impossible to conceive."

"Bradford once told me," Kate said, "that there are no thefts around here precisely because everyone knows that everyone has a gun, knows how to use it, and will use it."

"It does then, doesn't it," Grace asked, "sound rather as though someone would be likelier to grab a gun and shoot Mary Bradford out of sheer annoy-ance, rather than slip a bullet into someone else's gun? I mean, do you think this really sounds like a rural crime? It seems to me more the crime of a meta-phoric mind."

"A Joycean mind, you mean?" Lina asked.

"Literary, anyway."

"I don't follow that," Kate said. "It seems to me some rural type who hated her saw the chance of get-ting rid of her and took it. The fact that it would be involving a pack of nuts from the city in a hell of a lot of trouble simply added to the attractions of the method. Here comes a car."

The three of them stepped to the side of the road as the car, driven too fast by the inevitable adolescent male, slowed only enough to permit the yelling back of some invitation seething with sarcasm. As the three of them returned to the road, Grace chuckled.

"Now in a piece of mystery fiction, that car would contain not howling adolescents, but adventure. Do you read mystery stories?"

"Certainly," Kate said. "And do Double-Crostics. It's either that, I've found, or bridge, boats and skiing. Why?"

"It is interesting," Grace said, "how unlike life those stories really are. Their whole point is that so much *happens*. I don't mean those Ian Fleming books. Even nice little English mysteries, of what Auden calls the body in the vicarage type, they're so full of *events*. We have had a murder, now, but all we do, of course, is talk about it, and walk down a road together, three odd ladies in tennis shoes, to watch the husband of the deceased milk some cows."

"I know what you mean," Kate said. "The English mystery begins with someone reading one of those advertisements in the *Times,* on the front page where they used to be so eccentric as to put them, and it says, 'Peter, if you are wondering about me, go and see Henry. Colin.' So Peter rushes off to see Henry, who turns out to be an old nanny aged eighty, and the next thing you know he's trapped in some house behind the Iron Curtain, climbing out by hammering a piece of metal into the brickwork over and over again. If anybody locked me into a house, which is of course highly unlikely, I'd stay until I was rescued or, more likely, die of starvation."

"That was a very good book all the same."

"Of course it was a good book. Then there was the one I read recently of a thirty-fiveish spinster who goes to Europe for a vacation, has her car used for smuggling something or other into France, ends up locked in a cellar with some marvelous Frenchman, and takes the opportunity to learn what sleeping with men is all about, while the criminals are dropping bodies into the ocean the while."

"That was a very good book too."

"Excellent. But the point, I think, is that things don't happen to people who've lived thirty-five years or more without their happening."

"You're right," Grace said. "If I'd been locked in the cellar at age thirty-five with a Frenchman, however fascinating, I would have ended discussing some abstruse point of medieval culture if he was educated, or letting him tell me about the perils of the French economy and Gallic bravery in wars if he wasn't. Either one is the sort to whom adventure happens, or one isn't. And if one is the sort, I suspect one doesn't think or talk or read very much, one just adventures."

"One is certainly not likely to be locked in the cellar with a fascinating Frenchman," Lina said.

"And if we were, we would be so distressed at the thought of all those bodies being dropped into the ocean, we would not be thinking about having experiences."

"I would," Lina said.

"The whole point about mysteries," Grace said, "is that it is so nice to read about other people's doing things without having to do that sort of thing oneself."

"We are the sort who read mysteries and make memoranda," Kate said, smiling.

They had arrived at the barn. Bradford was milking, helped by the farmer from down the road.

"Do you mean they milk with machines?" Lina said, looking about her.

"They do everything with machines," Grace said. "I've gathered that much."

"Do the cows like standing with their heads caught that way?" Lina asked, after the visiting ladies, properly introduced, had, together with Kate, offered their condolences.

"Since they're fed that way, they like it," Bradford said, "but the new theory is that they're better off in open-pen barns, with a milking room and no stanchions. Watch out now." He reached above their heads and opened a trapdoor in the ceiling. A bale of hay came tumbling down from the hayloft above. He untied it and began raking the hay out to the cows.

"Mr. Bradford," Kate said. "Is there any way we can help with your children? We'll be glad to take them home with us for supper, and to sleep, if that would help you in any way."

"Thank you," Bradford said. "That's very kind. But a young lady from the village, friend of the family, has come out to look after things."

"Well," Kate said, "let me know if there's anything at all we can do."

The three ladies watched as Bradford fed the calves with powdered milk dissolved in water, removed the milking machine from each cow, fed each cow varying amounts of grain, and listened with a practiced ear to the machinery in his milk house. There a large, stainless steel tank, he explained to them, cooled the milk in three minutes from the cow's body temperature, about a hundred degrees, to less than sixty degrees. Three times a week the milk truck siphoned the milk out of the tank directly into the truck and drove away with it.

"Amazing," Grace said. "Is the whole top of the barn filled with hay?"

"It will have to be full soon, for the winter," Bradford said. "The hay we just fed the cows is the last of last summer's crop. There are over four thousand bales of hay in there already, and more to come. Would you like to see the hay elevator work?" he asked.

"Well," Grace Knole said, "if you would be so good."

"Please don't trouble," Kate said at the same time.

"No trouble," Bradford seemed glad to take his time explaining. "Those bales in the wagon," he said, "were thrown up there by the baling machine. We take each bale out of the wagon and put it on this elevator, which lifts it up to the hayloft. Watch out now." He started the machinery, and the elevator lifted the bale of hay up to the second story of the barn. Bradford, leaping to the hayloft before the bale, lifted it from the elevator and threw it back in the hayloft. "Come up and see," he said.

The three ladies eyed the perpendicular ladder leading to the hayloft with varying concern. Lina and Kate, without much hesitation, scrambled up it. Grace Knole remained on the ground. "I no longer admit," she said, "the possibilities of *either* cellars or haylofts. Look around, and tell me about it." Kate and Lina were astonished at the size of the barn's second floor. There was not a support or column visible; only open space and thousands of bales of hay. "It's a beautiful building," Kate said to Bradford.

"Designed it myself. Mary thought I was crazy, but I said it was possible to design an absolutely open hayloft. Poor Mary," he said, remembering. The three of them climbed solemnly down.

"One man," Grace said, as they started back up the road, "can run a farm, provided he is a mechanical genius, an architect, an agronomist, and a veterinarian rolled into one."

"What an extraordinary amount of hay," Lina said.

"On the whole," Kate said, "should one run into a Frenchman, I think a cellar would be preferable. Less irritating to the nasal passages, and less likely to induce acrophobia."

Reed was waiting for them halfway up the road. "Where have you been?" he asked. "You're not supposed to wander off from the scene of a murder without permission."

"Do you mean we're under house arrest?" Grace asked.

"We were exploring haylofts," Kate said.

"Find anything?"

"I should hate," Kate said, "to have to find anything in a hayloft. Bradford seems something less than inconsolable."

"I couldn't help wondering," Lina said, "about the girl from the village."

"Has Mr. Stratton asked Mr. Mulligan about Joyce?" Kate asked.

"What in God's name," Reed said, "is 'Ivy Day in the Committee Room'?"

"He *has* been asking about Joyce. What about 'Ivy Day'?"

"It seems Mr. Mulligan didn't know about something going 'Pop.' But then, of course, neither did I."

"But you haven't written several books on form and function in modern fiction."

"It's odd about Mr. Mulligan," Grace said.

9

Clay

By Sunday night, the police squads had finished. The mortal remains of Mary Bradford had been removed. "And where her immortal remains may be, I scarcely dare to think," Emmet observed. Mr. Stratton departed, together with his associate now dubbed M'Intosh.

On Monday, William was due for arraignment in the county court. Reed offered to drive him down, and Lina, for whose company William now manifested an almost childlike need, went along. They were to be met in court by John Cunningham, who would bring, Reed astonished everyone by saying, five thousand dollars in cash or certified check. "Cunningham's certain that's absolutely the highest bail they can set," Reed told Kate. "In fact," he continued, "if it's that high, it doesn't bode well for William if the police fail to find the murderer."

"But William hasn't committed murder," Kate said.

"He has, my dear. Accidental murder, but murder nonetheless."

"No more than if I ran over someone in my car, and killed her."

"In both cases, you see, the victim would be dead at the hand, so to speak, of another."

"Reed. Where is Cunningham getting the five thousand dollars? Does he provide it as part of his legal services?"

"May I live to see the day. The money is put up by the prisoner, or his friends, who will get it back if he doesn't vanish."

"I'm certain William doesn't have five thousand dollars."

"William doesn't have five thousand cents; not, that is, to spare."

"Reed, it's clearly my responsibility . . ."

"Which I, temporarily, am assuming."

"I can't see why you should come all over gallant."

"Neither can I. If you insist on immuring yourself in the woods, setting up a household which startles even the most hardened criminal lawyer in Boston, and then strewing the countryside with bodies, there is no good reason under the sun why I shouldn't let you find bail for your unfortunate employees, or leave them to battle their own way out of this predicament. After all, they must have known what they were letting themselves in for when they went to work for you. However, since I am not only as besotted as you are, but entangled into the bargain as a prime witness, if not a suspect, you must let me take upon my manly shoulders what responsibilities I can. In short, be of good cheer, have a drink waiting, should we return, and pray that the judge lets our William off with bail. This news, and more, will I bring upon my return; now, I to county courthouse, and thee to Araby, as they insist on saying in those dreary Shakespearean histories."

"They are *not* dreary."

"Good. Let us hope we get out of this mess soon enough to go and see one in Central Park. Odds bodkins!"

*   *   *

It was, therefore, a diminished group which settled down to lunch. Leo was off at camp, receiving the instruction of Mr. Artifoni. "Doubtless," Kate said, passing around the salad, "he will lecture the boys on the finer points of treating gunshot wounds. With luck, we will learn tonight whether one dies faster of a bullet in the head or the heart."

"I thought it was a sports camp," Grace said. "Is treating gunshot wounds a sport?"

"Every American boy should know first aid, my dear lady," Emmet said. "Surely you can grasp that. If, like me, he faints at the sight of blood, and doesn't know artificial respiration from Cheyne-Stokes breathing, he is clearly going to be of no use in emergencies, or so Leo informs me. I pointed out that boys are by definition no use in emergencies, but Leo said you never can tell. That's it, you see, Mr. Artifoni has all those little creatures positively longing for a calamity. Had Mary Bradford bled to death, I should have suspected half the camp of doing it to provide tourniquet practice. I'm virtually certain Leo's nightly prayer is that William or I will sever an artery and he can save us. Our dinner conversation is of the goriest, isn't it, Kate? Were it up to me, I would forbid the child to mention so much as a corpuscle. Does that answer your question?"

Grace grinned at him. "Mr. Crawford, I must arrange for you to address the master's students on Jane Austen, just so that I can come and listen to you."

"James Joyce, please, or someone equally modern. I've been reading through such scads of material, all of it marvelous, that I'm thinking of throwing over dear old Jane and writing on the importance of editors to modern literature. With Kate's permission, of course."

"Someone *ought* to do a book on Sam Lingerwell. How far have you got now?" Kate asked.

"It's scandalously slow going. Lingerwell did at least arrange the letters chronologically, which is to say each September he took out another huge file box and as he answered them, started throwing in all the

letters he received. It would have been much easier,
needless to say, for me to arrange the stuff by date
rather than correspondents, but that would scarcely
be of as much use to scholars. The Lawrence letters
are fascinating, but the Joyce letters are the ones
which really show up Lingerwell. Particularly the letters about *Dubliners*. After the *Portrait,* and with
Ulysses under way, he wrote Lingerwell rather less.
But the trouble they gave him over *Dubliners,* you
wouldn't believe it. What the printers particularly ob-
jected to, apparently, was the fact that he mentioned
real places in Dublin. Can you imagine? Today, if an
author doesn't mention real places, he might just as
well be writing for the funny papers. All he has to do
is say 'any similarity to an actual person or place is
purely coincidental' and everyone knows it's a *roman
à clef.*"

"Wasn't there something there shouldn't have been
about Edward VII?" Grace asked.

"How you do pick up information," Kate said.

"Well, why shouldn't he have something to say
about that fat voluptuary?" Emmet asked. "I know, I
know, you are going to tell me Edward brought about
the *entente* with France, whatever that was. But he
just managed it because he spoke perfect French. The
French, who are devoid of any moral sense, can't help
admiring a man who speaks their precious language
well. He still spent all his time enjoying himself in a
childish way."

"I have always liked him," Grace said. "Admittedly
he hated abstract ideas or intelligent conversation, and
apparently threw a fit if one was dressed a shade less
than impeccably. But he had great tact. He was once
visited by an Indian prince who, after eating asparagus, threw the stalks over his shoulder onto the carpet.
The other guests all stared at him in hopeless fascination, but old Tum-tum just started throwing *his* stalks
over his shoulder, as though it were the most natural
thing in the world, and soon all the guests were doing
it. I like tact on that scale."

"Better than his mother, anyway," Kate said, "who

is supposed to have been unreasonably upset when some visiting potentate sacrificed a sheep on one of the best rugs in Buckingham Palace."

"Tum-tum?" Emmet asked.

"That, I understand, is what his mistresses called him," Grace said. "I have to admit, you know, that in addition to being fond of Edward VII, I think *Dubliners* exceedingly overrated. I was looking at it last night, after our particularly fascinating session with Mr. Stratton. If half the Ph.D.'s in the country hadn't taken it upon themselves to write endlessly about the book, I don't think anyone would have paid it more than passing attention."

"That's what I've always felt about Milton," Kate said. "Once you've read *Paradise Lost* fourteen times, you damn well *have* to find it interesting."

"I don't agree, as you know," Grace said. "But I do not mean to disparage Joyce. I'm only suggesting that *Dubliners* is of real interest only because it led to *Ulysses*."

"To put it another way," Emmet said, *"Dubliners,* being Dublin without Bloom, never quite finds real life, as opposed to real death."

"We were saying something like that yesterday afternoon to those two gallants. Isn't it rather heartless," Kate went on, "speaking of how awful Dublin was, for us to be sitting around gossiping about Joyce with a woman recently dead on our doorstep?"

"Some," Emmet said, "we know to be dead though they walk among us; some are not yet born though they go through the forms of life; others are hundreds of years old though they call themselves thirty-six. I can't think why they should occur to me in connection with Mary Bradford; perhaps it's only in connection with you."

"That quote's never from Joyce."

"No," Emmet said. "I prefer lady authors, really; their wisdom is somehow distilled by the purity of their perceptions."

"Wow!"

"Do you like it? I thought it up for a beginning sentence of an essay."

"And where did you find that about some we know to be dead though they walk among us?"

"Virginia Woolf. Pity Lingerwell never corresponded with her. Now if you had any Woolf letters, you wouldn't see me for the dust."

"Emmet, don't joke about such things. The question is, what are we going to do about Mary Bradford?"

"You're not suggesting first aid after all this time?"

"I'm suggesting, not to put too fine a point on it, that if we don't find out who put the bullet in that gun, William's life is not going to be very easy, and I gather it isn't a bed of roses even now."

"Nobly spoken," Emmet said. "I, too, though you may not think it, have grown fond of William, and indeed have suggested that he apply to you for permission to desert Gerard Manley Hopkins, magnificent poet that he is, and write his dissertation on some of Lingerwell's material. But I'm afraid his block is psychological if not sexual; his whole life, really, is one long orgy of continence. Having committed murder, however unintentional, does not appear to me precisely the method one would choose above all others to help him over the double hurdle of dissertation block and rigid chastity. But what can we do? You are not, I trust, suggesting that we find a rural type and frame him?"

"I am suggesting," Kate said, "if I'm to be brutally honest, that we at least allow ourselves to assume it is a rural murder, and look for a rural murderer. I hope —indeed, I trust—that we shall be able to keep an open mind in the face of any evidence. At the same time I would rather like to find some evidence. The police, with a single-mindedness that is rather typical of them, appear to be concentrating their powers, on which I am not inclined to place too high a value, on our own poor selves."

"Well," Emmet said, "looking on what we know of this rural community as so much clay, let us see if we can design ourselves something of particularly clever construction."

"To continue your figure, it's rather a small amount of clay we have."

"Araby is a small town."

"Can we be certain the murderer is from Araby?"

"I rather think so. Of course, someone may have told someone, who told someone, who told someone in Detroit, who came all the way east to do the murder, but I can't help feeling that the neatness of the whole plan involved a particularly local familiarity with the conditions."

"Might I," Grace said, "ask a thoroughly tactless question?"

"By all means," Kate said. "But while we're mentioning tact, let me grasp the opportunity to say that there isn't the smallest reason why you should stay here. I'm delighted you agreed to come for a visit, and should I ever again take a house, which is about as likely as that I will allow myself to be launched in a spaceship, I should be delighted if you would honor me by being my guest. Meantime, however, I shouldn't blame you if you decided to get the hell out of here. If Lina wants to hold William's hand . . ."

"And I'd be surprised if he lets her go that far," Emmet said.

"Someone," Kate continued, ignoring Emmet, "will be glad to drive you home. I love you, I love having you, but please don't feel you have to stay, on the same theory which induced King Edward to throw the asparagus over his shoulder."

"Nothing could induce me to go. Unless you feel you can no longer bear my company, or find my presence, under the circumstances, the poverbial straw."

"Nonsense."

"Then let us say no more about it. I accepted your invitation, you know, not only because I like going places since I retired, and because dear Lina was driving up anyway, but also to serve my own ends. Should you ever become extricated from this preposterous situation, Kate, I would like to talk to you about something rather special."

"How enticing. Let's go to it immediately after lunch."

"Certainly not. First things first. I insist, since I'm to remain, on asking my thoroughly tactless question."

"Ask away."

"Are we certain that it was William who shot the woman? Or was it, possibly, Leo, for whom William is assuming the blame or, more exactly, shouldering the burden of inevitable guilt."

"Naturally," Kate said, staring into her coffee cup, "that occurred to me, right off like a shot, to be perfectly frank. I taxed William with being a chivalrous idiot, and suggested, with more forcefulness than delicacy, that I had never noticed lying to be a help, however gallant the lie, however compromising the circumstances. William agreed with me most sweetly, and assured me that he, in fact, had taken the gun from Leo and fired it. Leo, whom naturally I didn't want to interrogate too closely, seemed to agree with this account. My own suspicion, for what it's worth, is that William convinced Leo that he, William, had shot the lethal weapon when Leo had actually done so. A case, you might say, of brainwashing. Leo thinks the world of William, and would gladly accept William's word, forcefully enough presented, against the evidence of his own senses. But whether William is actually telling the truth, or protecting Leo, we may never know. Clearly, it's impossible, at this point, to pursue the matter any further."

"For some reason," Grace said, "I think it's important."

"Of course it's important. Apart from everything else, I have assumed, albeit unwillingly, summer custody of my nephew, only to involve him in a murder case, if not in the actual murder. What I shall say to my brother I scarcely dare to think."

"You haven't, I take it, heard from him."

"Fortunately, he is in Europe, and it is to be hoped that the European edition of the *Times,* which he is

almost certainly reading, will not carry the story of
our relatively minor rural murder. But a day of reck-
oning will come. I shall have to arm myself with a stiff
brandy and say 'I told you so.' I don't know what I
told him, but I always find that statement leaves the
opposition searching for the retort glorious, during
which hiatus one departs from the scene of combat.
I'm worried about Leo, naturally, but that's mostly
because it seems a worrying sort of situation. In point
of fact, he's done wonderfully well this summer,
though whether due to the presence of William, the
absence of his parents or the simple transformations
of time I couldn't say."

"Thank you for letting me get that off my mind,"
Grace said. "Let us return then to our clay, as Emmet
called it. Araby. How small is it?"

"About four hundred, including babes in arms.
About one hundred and forty odd households, I think,
pay taxes. Of these, well over half are summer people with large, highly taxed establishments, who do
not use the schools, the nursing service or the library
—which, incidentally, I have discovered to be a fancy
name for a few tattered volumes available between
the hours of two on Thursday."

"What made Sam Lingerwell ever decide to buy a
house here?"

"A good question it only recently occurred to me to
ask. I've written a letter to his daughter, and with luck
may get answers to a number of things. The reason,
however, is probably simply that he visited here and
liked the country. *We* know that the rural community
is not exactly to the taste of the urban devotee, but
that was hardly likely to emerge on a casual weekend.
The views are beautiful, the air cool, and somehow
country life seems so simple when one is contemplat-
ing it from a New York office in the middle of a frantic afternoon. He certainly couldn't have known, for
instance, that Mary Bradford would be a neighbor."

"Well, then," said Emmet, getting down to it, "who
have we in Araby who might have put the bullet in
William Lenehan's gun? There's us, the Bradfords,

Mr. Mulligan, Mr. Artifoni and his camp—who else can we mold into a suspect nearer to the heart's desire?"

"North of us, all summer people whom, alas, I am inclined to exonerate. They haven't 'called,' as the country people say; they certainly wouldn't know anything about the household—anyway, not enough to slip a bullet into the gun. Doubtless they've heard gossip about us from some of the natives, but that's always wildly off the mark—certainly impossible for all murder-planning purposes. That leaves the local people on the road, who of course include the Pasquales and the Monzonis, both of which families know all about us and are prime suspects. But did they hate Mary Bradford, really hate her? Make a note, Emmet, we must find out. Of course there are other farmers, and one or two Italian families to whom Mary Bradford always referred as 'white trash,' but apart from the fact that they are cheerful and improvident, like the Flopsy bunnies, I know little about them. I'm beginning to find this conversation depressing. More and more suspicion on poor us."

"Not necessarily," Emmet said. "Personally, I'm counting heavily on Mr. Mulligan. Who knows how close Mary Bradford was to the truth in her talk of orgies. And while Mr. Mulligan clearly has tenure, and is a full professor at a relatively young age, because he's published so much, one can be fired from a tenure position for moral turpitude."

"Surely that means raping a student in the halls, at the very least."

"Running orgies might do in a pinch. Or seducing young assistant professors. Even if Mr. Mulligan only thought Mary Bradford was a threat, won't that do? Then there's Artifoni, into whose affairs I would dearly love to look. Oh, stop worrying about Leo, Kate, I'm sure he's righteous as all get-out with small boys, but how much was the woman affecting his camp? Also, I don't want to cast aspersions in these matters, if they are aspersions, but Americans might do well to wake up to the fact that homosexual men who deeply resent women are not absolutely always those who go about prancing like little fawns. My suspicions, were I inclined to have any, would certainly be directed at men who spend their whole working time directing boys' activities, their whole playtime at games for boys, their spectator time watching male sports, and if they marry, always have five little crew-cut sons. I bet they drown the girls at birth. Mary Bradford may not have figured all this out, but who knows what her suspicions were. That woman had a nose for scandal, you have to give her that."

"Emmet, are you suggesting that I have not only exposed my nephew to murder, but have placed him in a camp filled with queers?"

"Relax. In point of fact, if Artifoni killed Mary Bradford, it was probably something to do with his precious camp. I'm merely trying to suggest that the most wholesome people may in fact have the personality for murder, which we ought to keep in mind should it be impossible to pin the murder on Artifoni for other reasons."

"Your language leaves much to be desired."

"Why not look at it the other way?" Grace said. "What possible motive could anyone in this house have for killing her? For one thing, the body would be unmistakably on their doorstep. For another, however huge a nuisance she was, and I gather that can scarcely be exaggerated, no one here had to kill her to keep her out of his life. At the worst, this summer's end would conclude any conceivable reason for further relationship. For a third, would anyone among us so stage a murder that a child or his tutor would become the instrument of death? It speaks of a lack of imagination for which I find no evidence here."

"None of this applies if it was Mrs. Monzoni or Mr. Pasquale."

"True. Clearly that needs following up. But this discussion does mean we must look at Mr. Mulligan, I agree with that. Orgies or no orgies, Lina's evidence, should she give it, certainly indicates some lack of imagination on Mr. Mulligan's part."

"How do both of you know so much about Lina and Mr. Mulligan?" Kate asked.

"The Lord hath given us eyes; should we see not?" Grace said. "There were moments when those pleasant summer people were telling me about artificial insemination, and the marvelous indications of the proper time for insemination established by the cows' mounting one another—you may well look amazed, my dear, but I have noticed people often rejoice in discussing sex under the aegis of agriculture—there were moments during this enlightening discourse when I really thought Mr. Mulligan was going to do a little mounting himself, right there in his living room."

"Professor Knole, I'm shocked," Kate said.

"I too," said Emmet.

"The trouble with you two," Grace said, "is that like all young people, you wish to restrict the benefits of what I believe is called frank language to your own cohorts. I have often thought we who are more mature should let you hear how it sounds on the lips of another generation. More coffee, anyone?"

10

Eveline

The courthouse contingent returned just before dinner, sore-footed and world-weary, calling loudly for drink and sustenance.

"I thought perhaps you would bring John Cunningham back with you?" Kate said to Reed.

"Frankly," Reed said, "we can't afford it."

"Doesn't he have any nonbusiness hours he just gives away?"

"Not he. At least, not when he's got any cases pending, and I guess that's constantly, to all intents and purposes. Don't be hard on him, Kate. He took a lot more time to turn up in court in Pittsfield today than he would have done for many clients paying double the fee. And a jolly good thing too. I've brought you a present, by the way."

"Why was it a jolly good thing? You're terrifying me."

"I better have a martini on the rocks. Our only meal was a soggy sandwich and Coca-Cola, neither my favorite forms of food. I am either too old or too degenerate to get a lift from Coke. Thank you. Do serve Lina and William too; their need is greater than mine. Take my advice, dear girl, and don't play around with guns. We had, of course, to pull a judge whose grandson had just shot off his own foot."

"Reed, how frightful!"

"It's not supposed to be anything else. Guns are the devil and all, I've always thought so. But poor William was feeling bad enough in all conscience, without having the judge lecture him at great length, holding up an already overcrowded court calendar into the bargain. I thought he would make William write a hundred times over 'I never again will touch a gun.' "

"It's I who should write something over and over," Kate said. "I've always loathed and detested guns. But I was afraid of impinging upon a masculine prerogative. Also, I'd read *Hedda Gabler* at perhaps too impressionable an age. Let's face it, modern Freudian lingo has got us so frightened of appearing to be castrating women that we won't even take a gun away from a boy. And I do not want to hear a chuckle out of you, Emmet Crawford."

"I haven't so much as uttered, dear lady. Proud enough am I to be drinking cocktails with the grownups."

"Well, this is a special day."

"May I have something with my tomato juice, Aunt Kate?" Leo asked, pleased at the break in routine which permitted William and Emmet and himself a place at the cocktail hour.

"I'll give you something in your tomato juice you won't like," Kate viciously said.

"Mr. Artifoni says . . ."

"I don't care if Mr. Artifoni forces gin down the throats of his gurgling charges, you cannot have anything in your tomato juice."

"Aunt Kate! To eat, I meant. Mr. Artifoni says that no good athlete ever drinks or smokes or . . ." Leo interrupted himself to reach for a handful of nuts.

"Or what, for the sake of the blessed saints?" Emmet asked.

"Or stays up past ten o'clock," Leo concluded. "Good athletes never see 'The Late Late Show.'"

"What else happened in court?" Grace asked.

"I'll spare you the technicalities and the long, dreary hours, the spirit-defeating atmosphere. William was arraigned and released on payment of bail." Reed paused as Emmet, at a sign from Kate, led Leo from the room. William and Lina had already departed. "Let us pray," Reed continued, "that William does not consider pulling a Lord Jim and fleeing his conscience all over the tropics, because riding on that lad is more money than I'd care to lose. I must say, Eveline was a great support in time of need. She even cheered me up, which was well beyond the call of duty."

"What will happen if William is found guilty of murder in whatever degree it properly is?"

"Who knows? Perhaps a suspended sentence. Let's hope it doesn't come to that."

"The simple fact is," Kate said, "we have to find the real murderer."

"Kate," Reed said. "I cannot bear to have you hatching some plot that would give the Hardy boys pause. Let's face the fact that it's almost impossible to find out who put the bullet in that gun. All we can do is stir up a peck of trouble and probably get the lot of us run out of the country. Not that I'd mind."

"Reed, believe it or not, I haven't a clue as to how to put a bullet in a gun. Maybe there are others with similar alibis, and by a process of elimination . . ."

"We'll have no one left in Berkshire County who isn't aiming a rifle at *your* head. Kate, I beg of you, behave."

"Won't the policemen do anything?"

"Everything, as is the dull lot of policemen. But what you've got to recognize is that, unless the police are absolutely overwhelmed with evidence to the contrary, they're inclined to assume that the man who pulled the trigger is the murderer. They are certainly not going to run around like one of your favorite detectives proving by some esoteric mumbo jumbo that would never stand up in court—which is why the culprit always commits suicide—that so-and-so must have done it because the gun, by some miraculous idiosyncrasy known only to two people, will shoot a bullet only if the Lord's Prayer is murmured over it in Sanskrit on three successive rainy nights. If you absolutely forced another martini on me, I might acquiesce with a fair grace. Speaking of grace, you never asked me what was the present I brought you."

"I hope it's a proper clue which will lead inevitably to the solution of all our problems."

"That remains to be seen. What I brought you is the collected works, or at least as many as I could collect on short notice, of our Mr. Mulligan. It transpired, during one of those soggy-sandwich repasts about which I was wringing your withers a while back, that Pittsfield, bless its up-to-date little heart, has a community college and a bookstore. So while the court was recessed, Cunningham was on the phone, and William and Eveline seemed capable, under pressure, of getting along without me, I wandered round to the bookstore and discovered that many of Mr. Mulligan's books are available in paperback. The clerk told me they were very popular with students, mainly, he intimated, because they were such good 'cram stuff'— his phrase, not mine. Anyway, since you and Grace Knole keep saying you're interested in Mr. Mulligan, I thought you might want to cast a professional eye on whatever it is has got him a promotion to full professor and all the rest of it. Considering, I mean, that he didn't know what went 'Pop' in the committee room."

"Who's hatching plots now, my little Hardy boy?"

"That's the thanks I get for bearing gifts. Another? I couldn't possibly. Force it down my throat."

"Dibs on *Form and Function in Modern Fiction*," Grace said, looking over the package of books.

"By all means," Kate said. "I shall confine myself to *The Novel: Tension and Technique*. Much more my cup of tea anyway."

"Dinner, dinner, dinner," Leo called, "Mrs. Monzoni said so."

"And what of interest did Mr. Artifoni say today, my little man?" Emmet asked as they were seated at the table.

"Mr. Artifoni said that guard is the most important position in basketball, even if he doesn't get to shoot baskets and it doesn't seem so important at first. He said," Leo went on, helping himself generously to mashed potatoes, "that the guard doesn't talk of how many baskets *he* got, but of how many baskets his man got."

"How many baskets did your man get?" Kate asked.

"He didn't," Leo said. "We never play basketball on Mondays. Please pass the pickles."

William and Eveline, after suitable apologies, had departed for supper in town, doubtless to consume the same sort of veal cutlets with which Kate had entertained Reed on his first night in the country. They returned at something after ten o'clock, apparently having undone whatever bonds of sympathy they had woven since the murder. William went upstairs to bed, pleading a fatigue which certainly was likely enough, while Lina threw herself in front of the fire and began guzzling brandy in an ominous manner. Reed, too, had retired, Emmet was at work, as ever, on the letters which were becoming something close to a passion with him, Grace Knole was upstairs, presumably settling down for the night, and Kate resigned herself to a discussion of the perils of womanhood.

"I expect you're damn sick of the lot of us," Lina said. "And small reward I am to you, for inviting me for a visit, or rather, permitting me to invite myself. I'd better take myself off in the morning. I cannot image," she viciously added, "where the idea that men are the aggressors in sex ever arose from. Shrinking violets are nothing to it."

"So Shaw always insisted. At the same time, there *is* Mr. Mulligan."

"How horribly, hideously true. Can it be that men

merely object to the entanglements of love, not to sex itself?"

"Dylan Thomas, as I remember, propounded some such theory. But then he was clearly not the best example of monogamous manhood, however good a poet."

"William's monogamous. He loves one only: himself."

"What exactly is William's problem? Sin?"

"I think so. And the fact that he thinks he can't possibly marry, financially speaking. I don't think he really minds that I have a Ph.D. and he doesn't yet, but he does mind not being able to get to work on his dissertation, and finding it all grind when he does get down to it, and not very likely to be interesting in the end."

"In the Victorian period, of course, when muscular Christianity was popular, people like Carlyle would recommend work and cold baths."

"Exactly William's theory, evidently. He keeps plodding at Hopkins' inscapes, and takes long cold swims in the ocean when he's home. I am not Victorian, thank the lord. My feeling is, if a man has so much energy he wants to swim halfway to Europe, why not put the energy to good use and go to bed with someone? What *has* he been doing here to sublimate, now he's so far from the ocean, besides pretending to shoot guns?"

"He plays with Leo, climbs mountains, swims in the pool. He's even been known to play tennis with me once or twice. Lina, is there some reason why it has to be William? Can't you, according to the old bromide, be friends and find your love life somewhere else?"

"I could, of course. As you know, to my shame, I've even considered being seduced, if not actually attacked. But in the end, it's always William, blast him. I mean, we seem to be right together about so many things. And in all the years I've known him, he's never found anyone else either. And one thing about William, he sticks to his principles. I mean, he isn't one of those with pure girls on one hand and loose women on the other, which is so often, I fear, supposed to be a failing of religious young men. I mean, he really *believes* in chastity."

"If that's so, then why not stop brooding and put your mind to something else—writing a book, perhaps, or taking a trip around the world, if you prefer that. You're wonderfully free, you know. Does it frighten you to look at it in that light?"

"I'm not independent like you, Kate. I like doing things with people I know."

"Then stop having fantasies about sleeping with people you don't know—the masterful Italian, á la Mastroianni, met one dark night in Naples or on the Riviera."

"That's a low blow."

"Look, Lina. Life isn't replete with possibilities. For women who don't just naturally move into a house in the suburbs with husband and children and community activities, there are only three possible lives. You can marry and continue to function professionally, even with children. The number of this sort increaseth. Or, you can not marry, seeing a clear choice and choosing to work. This sort belongs, usually, to an earlier generation, like Grace Knole. Their number decreaseth. Or you can be one of that third group, much less publicized, which requires and enjoys the love of men, usually more than one man in a lifetime, and scorns the role of homemaker. There used to be lots of Frenchwomen of that sort who pined away when forced to spend any time at their chateaux."

"Like George Sand, you mean, or Madame de Staël?"

"If you insist on rather extreme examples. Or Madame du Châtelet—do you know Nancy Mitford's book on her? Or in this century, Doris Lessing. Simone de Beauvoir, Colette. As Doris Lessing put it in an interview, marriage is not one of the things she's good at."

"Are you in the third group?"

"It would appear so. Certainly running a house this summer has not improved my temper. The point, however, is that you are in one of the first two groups, probably the one who marries and continues with a profession. You wouldn't be a virgin in your late twenties otherwise, frankly, but who knows. Now don't open your little mouth to ask any questions about me, because I don't intend to answer them. Why not forget dreams of William, on the one hand, and dreams of wild nights with unknown lovers of infinite experience on the other, and settle down to work? Meeting the man with whom you could spend your life is as much serendipity as anything: it usually happens when you're worrying about something else. As to your taking yourself off in the morning, don't. Now, before you become absolutely blotto on brandy, would you mind telling me, in all the detail you can muster, what happened in court today?"

When, several hours later, Kate staggered upstairs with Lina in tow, and saw her headed in the general direction of bed and oblivion, she reached her own room with a sense of infinite relief, and a longing for solitude. But life appears to offer solitude only to those already burdened with too much of it. There was a knock on the door, and Grace Knole came in.

"You look exhausted," Grace said. "I've only poked my nose in to say good night, and to tell you that Mr. Mulligan has all the literary mastery of a preengineering student. But we can talk about that tomorrow."

"By all means. But do come in and tell me what that matter was you were hinting at so beguilingly at lunch."

"I'm afraid that's rather a long conversation, Kate. Tomorrow will do for that, too."

"Oh, come in and sit down, for heaven's sake. I told you all we do is talk—or were you telling me?—on the way to see the cows. Talk, talk and more talk, and some of it actually conversation. I do intersperse it, of course, with tennis and walks, and an occasional swim—but let's face it, if you want to know what a man likes, watch what he does. I talk."

"Interspersed also with a little lovemaking now and then?"

"Grace, I will not discuss sex with one other person this summer, and maybe not even next. What in God's name has got into you? Lina I can excuse—she's very twixt and tween, and simply brimful of indecisions. But what possible reason you can have . . ."

"Keep your shirt on. I do not intend to lay at your feet my personal burdens, if any. I merely wished to point out, somewhere along the way, that the president of Jay College probably wouldn't be able to have a lover. A husband, yes. Don't you think you smoke too much?"

"Certainly I smoke too much. I comfort myself with the thought that there's nothing like knowing what *kind* of cancer you're going to die from. Light up a cigarette and be *sure*. Grace, have you gone completely, ninety-nine point forty-four percent mad?"

"Very likely. Believe it or not, there's a shortage of really competent women around, let alone women who aren't married to men whose careers or egos foreclose any possibilities of their having a college president for a wife. Let's face it, Bunting may be the most prominent woman president around, she was even on the Atomic Energy Commission, but if her husband hadn't, most unhappily, died, she'd still probably be tutoring in chemistry somewhere. As for the unmarrieds, those who can hold their own in the world of college and university administration—as I said, you're probably too tired."

"I'm certainly too tired to be president of Jay College for Women. This is the first indication I've ever had that your powers were failing. Or have you simply developed an odd sense of humor? Jay College may be one of the oldest women's colleges in the country, and with a great reputation, but not even two hundred years of respectable history could survive me."

"Rave on. Just think about it. The trustees are, I

happen to know, prepared to make you an offer. They've done a lot of research on you, sat in on your classes, read your books . . ."

"You're positively making me blush. I haven't gone crimson like that . . ."

"Since the last person paid you a heartfelt compliment: You have many drawbacks, I don't mind telling you, and your inability to accept a compliment is certainly one of them. Also, you're somewhat less than a mountain of tact, you're impatient with brainlessness and the throwing around of weight, and while you have the greatest respect for manners and courtesy, you have none at all for the proprieties as such."

"I wonder you ever thought of me."

"Well, you know what Henry James wrote to a young acquaintance who had just met Edith Wharton: 'Ah my dear young man,' he wrote, 'you have made friends with Edith Wharton. I congratulate you; you may find her difficult, but you will never find her stupid, and you will never find her mean.' "

"That's nice, Grace. But hardly the qualifications for a college president, which, incidentally, I definitely don't want to be. Did you suggest me?"

"It might surprise you to know how many people suggested you. I've already given you the bit about the scarcity of capable women. I'm here this weekend, really, to sound you out—and to add to the soundings all the persuasions I can personally bring to bear which, as you know, I profoundly feel."

"Thank you. I'll try to take that compliment properly. But you know, were I asked for suggestions of people to be president, I'd suggest you. You'd be perfect, Grace."

"I agree with you, actually. And unlike you, I accept compliments with the greatest self-satisfaction and not the shade of a blush. But people these days want their college presidents young. To be frank, I can't imagine why. It seems to me that college presidents, like popes, ought to be old when appointed: they can then afford to take risks, and they can't live on too long and get set in their ways. That, however, is not the American way. They did ask me to serve pro tem, but I refused. All the headaches, and no power. Don't try to answer now. Perhaps I shouldn't have let this come up, with all this other problem hanging over your head—but I thought I'd give you another bone to gnaw on."

"Many thanks. Are you suggesting I marry in order to qualify for the job?"

"I'm suggesting nothing. Only trying to hint at the problems. But before you turn it down, Kate, remember, it's a position of power, and power is one of the most remarkable experiences there is."

"I've never wanted power."

"I know that. Exactly why you should take it, rather than someone who has always wanted it. Good night, Professor Fansler."

11

The Sisters

Kate had written, the day of the murder, to Sam Lingerwell's daughter, informing her of the catastrophe and asking as many questions as she could think of. Kate was not clear really whether she was apologizing or howling for help, but after writing the letter over four times—few letter-writing manuals include models for informing someone of murder—she finally sent the fifth version off without even bothering to reread it. Sister Veronica had answered by return:

Dear Kate:
 I was saddened by your letter, with its frightful news, and your kindness in underestimating the enormous burden to yourself. I have taken the liberty of mentioning the matter to the Mother Superior, and she has agreed that all the sisters shall say a special prayer for you. I trust we will not offend you with our prayers: I know that my father did not care for them. Poor Mr. Lenehan, who must bear the dreadful burden of having fired the gun, is most constantly in our prayers as in our hearts.

I feel myself enormously to blame. I ought not to have asked you to undertake so great a responsibility. If there is any way now in which I can proffer practical help, do please let me know of it. You will, I am certain, understand how impossible it was for me to cope with my father's papers, particularly since, to judge from the offers being urged on me at every turn, they could be the source of a good deal of scholarly work. But perhaps by now the greater work is finished, or will you merely smile that I should so underestimate the magnitude of the job? [Kate smiled.]

To answer your question, I am not certain why my father bought a house precisely where he did. In fact, I asked him that question the last time I saw him. It seems that some partner in his publishing firm, from which he had, as you know, more or less retired, had been used to visit a Mr. Mulligan in that part of the country. He was informed by Mr. Mulligan, and subsequently informed my father, of the house which was for sale, and which my father found attractive and subsequently bought. I am not certain, however, but I rather doubt, that Mr. Mulligan knew my father.

[Here followed some points about Kate's actual "renting" of the house.]

The other sisters here join me in my prayers for you. There is no way to thank you. But should you be enabled to stand up under this trial, it can but increase the gratitude I, as my father before me, must always feel toward you.

Dominus vobiscum

"So Mulligan knew Lingerwell was coming here," Reed said, when Kate had shown him the letter.

"She doesn't say that exactly. Sam Lingerwell did get here through Mr. Mulligan, but only indirectly."

"Interesting, just the same, that there was a connection."

"Interesting in more ways than one. Did it ever occur to you, Reed, to wonder how Mr. Mulligan manages to afford that house, and Mrs. Pasquale, and all, even on his income from his books and his salary as a professor—full, admittedly, but still, a professor?"

"In the first place he's a bachelor, and in the second place most teachers of literature have incomes additional to their salaries, or so you often tell me."

"True enough. But Mr. Mulligan happens to have mentioned to Lina, who told me, that he started as a very poor boy, and is still supporting his parents. So much for his bachelor freedom and his inherited income. He drives a Jaguar, has a swimming pool, together with all the filter machinery thereto, and it is no cheap matter to entertain houseguests, as I know to my cost, and Mr. Mulligan does it constantly."

"Kate, if you are trying to cast Mr. Mulligan in the role of first murderer, I positively forbid it. At least, cast away, but don't *do* anything about it. He may have the morals of a billy goat and the literary qualifications of General Eisenhower, but there is no reason . . ."

"Reed. Did you *read The Novel: Tension and Technique* before presenting it to me with all the airs of a man serving mangoes in January?"

"Naturally I didn't read it. Do I expect you to read the *Harvard Law Review?* Talk sense."

"Very well. Let me tell you then that Mr. Mulligan has contented himself with collecting a lot of tired clichés, if a cliché may ever be said to be without fatigue, and has simply written them all down in a most inept manner."

"You mean he can't write?"

"On the contrary, he writes with a certain felicity. He can't think."

"The man in the bookstore in Pittsfield said, as I'm sure I told you but you probably weren't listening, that they are very popular with students."

"For purposes of cramming, or, likelier still, plagiarizing papers. They sound undergraduate enough to be genuine, don't you get the point? Grace Knole found the same with the book she was reading."

"Look, Kate, I know you consider book publishing a profession second only in purity of soul to the Little

Sisters of Charity, but surely they are as happy to make money as anybody else. If the books sell, there's your answer."

"They sell only in cheap paperbacks, and then to college students. Furthermore, they sell in paperbacks not published by the Calypso Press."

"What's your point?"

"That it's really extraordinary that Calypso ever published these books in the first place, and in hard cover into the bargain. They have a college list that has the respect of every faculty and is the envy of every other college department in the publishing field. What's Mulligan doing on it?"

"I'm sure I don't know. Don't you think perhaps you're exaggerating the ineptitude of the books? After all, you don't read everything that's being published today."

"Heaven forfend."

"Well, there you are."

"Reed, I think I'll take a day or two off and drive down to New York, maybe have a talk with the people at Calypso. Being in charge of the Lingerwell papers should provide an excuse. Anyway, I can't stay around here very much longer without a small interlude, and this looks as good a chance as any. Will you lend me your Volkswagen?"

"What's the matter with your car, or rather your brother's? It's bigger and safer."

"Now don't come all over the protective male. I have to leave my car here for William or Emmet to drive and fetch Mrs. Monzoni, among other things. Of course, if you're feeling possessive about your beastly little bug, I'll rent a car, or have Emmet drive me to the train."

"Why not let me come with you?"

"Thank you, Reed, but would you rally round here and keep things afloat?"

"Meaning, as you always mean when you start talking like an ad agency, that you want to be alone to think, or some such nefarious activity."

"What an understanding man you are."

"I am not in the least understanding. I simply lack forcefulness and manly overbearance. Besides, if I go back to New York, the office will certainly develop a crisis, and I'll have to cut my vacation short."

"I'm sorry it hasn't been a better vacation."

"It has had its moments. When are you leaving?"

"This evening, I think, after dinner. Do you want to walk down to the vegetable garden with me? I want to ask Mr. Pasquale to take some zucchini over to Mrs. Pasquale to cook for supper for Mr. Mulligan."

"You may suspect him of murder, but you send around vegetables?"

"Naturally; one must be neighborly."

"Why not take them yourself and be really neighborly?"

"Because if I ask Mr. Pasquale to take them to Mrs. Pasquale, he will take enough for them to eat at home."

"Ah, you're catching on, I see, to rural life."

"There is no life, my dear Reed," Kate said in ponderous tones, "least of all the rural, without its mysterious rites and rituals. I will also send some corn and cucumbers."

12

After the Race

In point of fact, Kate greatly enjoyed driving the beastly little bug, as she had called it. True, one bounced about as though on a motorcycle, and the protection to be afforded, in a crash, by its beetle body, was certainly minimal; yet driving it, she felt that she and the car were working together, whereas with the huge automobile lent her by her brother, she seemed to be steering on gracious sufferance from the car itself.

Feeling, not without guilt, lighthearted, she turned onto the main route leading to the Taconic Parkway. She had decided to eschew the shortcuts in the interest of saving time: it would certainly be preferable to reach New York in time to call Ed Farrell, the present editor-in-chief at Calypso, and possibly even see him tonight. She had been unable to reach him on the phone before leaving Araby; the hope was that he would have returned, by eleven, should he have been out, as he so often was, at dinner with an author. Kate smiled in anticipation as she began to mount Smith Hill. The natives claimed this was a hill so high the wagons had to be emptied, in the old days, before the horses could pull them to the top, and it was the test of any old car to see if it could make the hill in third. A signal light was at the top of the hill, and Kate found an idiotic (and secret) delight in racing the car to see if she could get through the light before it changed to red. She began now to race. I ought not to speed in cars, she sternly told herself since, like Alice, she was in the habit of talking to herself with a certain severity. But the race against the light, which she barely sneaked through, exhilarated her. I expect I'll be driving a motorcycle next, she said, but not even this frightful thought could dampen her spirits. She remembered that Mr. Mulligan, who had stopped by late in the afternoon to thank her for the vegetables (nominally; in fact, he was on the lookout for tasty bits of news, or perhaps the chance to take a walk with Lina), had remarked that he always tried not to stop at the light at the top of Smith Hill, because if you got through that, and didn't meet up with an accident or the need for gas, you could make it all the way to the Saw Mill River without stopping, and on one glorious occasion he had made both lights on the Saw Mill and had got to the Henry Hudson Bridge without falling below thirty-five, except for tolls.

The country was more beautiful than ever in the evening light. The farms seemed set out on the hills, neatly plowed fields contrasting in shades of green with their adjoining meadows. Kate felt certain that the good life might somehow be possible here, yet knew this to be only a dream. A short time after the race for the light, she turned on the car's lights, seeing that many of the vehicles coming toward her had already done so. Night was approaching. The little bug trundled along in high. There was very little traffic on the Taconic Parkway. She had a feeling that she would be able to tell Mr. Mulligan she had matched his record. Suddenly a car shot out of a side road. Kate slammed on her brakes, and her car jerked to a halt. Cursing, Kate heard the car stall. She turned the starter. Silence. The motor was not turning over. The battery was dead. Damn, hell and corruption.

A car soon stopped, offering help. Kate asked only to be pushed to the side of the road, which the man rather gingerly did, the bumper of his large car not really meeting the bumper of the Volkswagen. "Sorry I can't be more help lady," he said. "I'm afraid I don't know anything about cars, particularly those little foreign ones. I'm the sort who calls a repairman if the television set becomes unplugged. *You* know."

"To be frank," Kate said, "I have frequently doubted whether anyone understands the internal combustion engine. Perhaps you would be kind enough to call for help, however, when you pass a phone?"

"Gladly," the man said. "Maybe you got a flat tire?"

"I don't think that would affect the battery, do you?"

"No, I guess not. Noticed your lights are very dim. You seem to know a lot about cars."

"Only what I learned from leaving the ignition on one long, sad night. But surely the battery ought to have been recharging all this time." The man waved an amiable hand and departed. Kate sat down on the roadside to wait. She was joined, before very long, by the state police.

"Anything wrong, lady?" they asked in tones which, if not discourteous, were certainly not brimming with graciousness either. Kate restrained an impulse to say she had given way to a desire to sit on the roadside and meditate.

"My battery appears to have gone dead," she said. "The motor won't turn over."

They greeted this analysis of the situation with all the skepticism due any woman who calls by name any of a car's inner accouterment.

They lifted the hood (I wonder if it's called a hood, Kate thought) at the back of the car, and gazed meaningfully into the engine. "Water in the fuel line?" one said. The other reached into the back seat and lifted the rear seat out. "Plenty of water in the battery," he said. "What about the gas filter?"

"That would scarcely affect the battery," Kate said, for the second time that evening. It was by now quite dark. The state troopers did not appear to appreciate her contributions to the discussion.

"Let's see your license and registration," one of them said. At that moment a repair truck, apparently summoned by the man who had pushed her to the side of the road, appeared.

"Hey, Mac," the trooper said. "See if you can figure out what's the matter here."

The repairman turned on the ignition and tried to start the car. Nothing happened. "Battery's dead," he said.

"My battery," Kate said, feeling more and more like someone who has been given only one line in a play and must keep repeating it in rehearsal after rehearsal, "should have recharged while I was driving."

"Your generator's probably gone," the repairman said. He extracted a long wire, with clips on either end, and began placing the tips mysteriously. "The minute you put on your lights you drew all your juice out of the battery. In most cars, there's an indicator on the dash to tell you. Not these babies."

"I wouldn't have noticed it anyway," Kate said.

"Your brushes are probably gone. Have to tow you in."

"My brushes?" Kate said.

"I've been patrolling this road a year now," the state trooper said. "No one ever had trouble with brushes."

"It's unusual to have the generator go in these cars. Particularly"—the repairman flashed a light at the speedometer—"in one that's gone only nine thousand miles. Very strange. These cars don't break down much. Have to tow you in."

"Just a minute," the state trooper said. "Your license and registration."

"Have I done anything wrong?" Kate asked. The state trooper, with his companion, waited stolidly, not deigning to answer. Kate reached into the car for her purse, into the purse for her wallet, into her wallet for her driver's license. It wasn't there.

"It must be," she said. "A New York State driver's license, quite up to date, with no convictions on it." From her wallet she carefully removed her faculty identification card, her university bookstore card, her faculty club card, her social security card, her Blue Cross card, a small calendar and three five-cent stamps. "It's always there," she said.

"It's an offense to drive without an operator's license. Let's see the registration."

Kate remembered Reed's voice: "The registration's here, in a plastic folder, in the map compartment. I keep it underneath. You'll have to show it," he had added with a frivolity which now seemed prophetic, "when they pick you up for reckless driving." She slid into the car and looked in the map compartment. The plastic folder was there, but no registration form was inside it.

"No registration," one state trooper told the other. Kate wondered, not for the first time, why all state policemen either are or appear eight feet tall and devoid of all human feelings. Probably their boots, she thought. And goggles.

"You'll have to come with us," they said.

"Do you mean in your police car?" She was ignored. The trooper turned to the repairman. "Can you haul that in?"

"Right. I could recharge the battery," he said, shrugging his shoulders, "and she might get started, but with the lights on, she wouldn't go far." He handed Kate a card.

"Get in," the trooper said. Kate got into the back of the police car, and one of the troopers got in the back with her, apparently to make certain she did not try to throttle the driver. "Is it a very bad offense to drive without a license?" she asked the trooper next to her. He did not answer. Evidently it was not his custom to converse with criminals.

At the state police station, Kate was told to wait.

She asked if she might telephone, but was again ignored. Then she was called to talk with an officer behind a desk.

"Why were you driving without a license?" he asked.

"Someone must have taken it out of my wallet."

"The same person who took the car's registration?"

"Apparently."

"Why should anyone do that?"

"I can't imagine. They couldn't have known I would have to stop, and if I hadn't stopped, you wouldn't have found out. So it can't have been a desire to cause trouble."

"Know anyone who'd want to cause you trouble?"

Kate shook her head.

"Got any identification with you?"

"All the identification cards from the university where I teach."

"Which university's that?"

Kate told him. It was clear his opinion of it, if any, had declined on learning of her association with it.

"Do you own the car you were driving?"

"No."

"Who does?"

There was a long, palpable pause while Kate did not answer the question. Should she give them Reed's name? On the surface of it, it seemed logical enough. They would call him in Araby and straighten out this whole dreadful mess. But Reed, after all, was an assistant district attorney, and reporters did look at police blotters. Anyway, if two people recently connected with a murder should now be in the hands of the police again, however innocently, would it not be one of those tangles which somehow, as time passes, become inexplicable in simple words? In any case, it certainly couldn't *help* Reed to be tied up in all this.

"Who owns it?" the officer asked again.

"I don't know," Kate said.

"You don't know. Do you mean you borrowed it, but you don't know from whom?"

"I didn't steal it," Kate said.

"Are you acquainted with the person you borrowed it from?"

"It's not that I don't know," Kate said, shifting her ground. "It's that I won't say."

"Take her inside," the officer said.

"Haven't I a constitutional right to make a phone call before you lock me up?" Kate asked.

"Everybody knows all about his constitutional rights today," the officer said. "Rights, rights, rights, for everybody but the police. You can make one phone call. In there."

One of the troopers led Kate into another room where a telephone stood on a table. She put in the call to Araby. It was answered, against her most fervent hopes by Leo. "Leo. This is Aunt Kate."

"Hi, Aunt Kate. You in New York already?"

"No, dear. Leo, will you let me speak to—" she glanced up at the trooper, who was watching her— "let me speak to the oldest man there." To the trooper, this sounded like just what he expected from a woman who had probably never had a driver's license, had eaten the registration, and done something hideous to the generator. So his looks implied.

"Mr. Pasquale's gone home."

"Not Mr. Pasquale, Leo. Staying in the house."

"I don't know who's older, William or Emmet. Wait, I'll ask."

"Leo!" But before Kate could stop him, he had dumped down the receiver in the way of small boys, and could be heard shouting in the distance.

"Hurry up," the trooper said.

"I'm having a little trouble finding him," Kate said. The trooper's look suggested that it wouldn't surprise him if she had trouble finding the Empire State Building on Thirty-fourth Street and Fifth Avenue in the blaze of the noonday sun.

"William's older," a breathless Leo reported. "Funny your wanting to know their ages now you're gone. Emmet's birthday . . ."

"Leo. Please. Let me speak to the man who isn't William or Emmet."

"Is this a game? Mr. Artifoni says . . ."

"Leo. Please."

"O.K., O.K." The receiver crashed down again. After what seemed only a little longer than forever, while Kate resolutely refused to meet the eyes of the trooper, Reed's voice could be heard.

"Kate? Where on earth are you?" No voice, Kate thought to herself, no voice ever sounded so beautiful.

"I'm in a police station. State police. The car registration's gone, along with my driver's license, and something ghastly's happened to the generator." She realized her voice sounded as panicky as she felt. Ridiculously, she recalled a *New Yorker* cartoon of long ago in which a woman is telephoning from a police station: "Henry," she is saying, "I did something wrong on the George Washington Bridge."

"Where are you?"

"Where am I?" Kate asked the trooper. He told her.

"All right, I'm coming, in your brother's scorned limousine. Let me talk to someone there."

"I didn't give them your name. I was afraid . . ."

"I respect your noble silence. Let me talk to the officer in charge, if possible."

"I don't know if they'll let you. They were going to put me in a cell." Kate looked up at the trooper. "He wants to talk to you," she said. The trooper looked dubious, but he took the phone.

So Kate, only slightly to her disappointment, didn't wait in a cell after all. She waited in the waiting room for Reed's arrival which, she decided, could not be in less than an hour.

He arrived in forty-five minutes, however, having driven the limousine, one supposed, at close to eighty. Kate hoped to remember in calmer times to ask him if he had made the Smith Hill light.

"Here I am in the clink," Kate said. "Oh, frabjous day. The question is, as I figured out while waiting for you, what am I accomplishing by being here, or, more exactly, what am I not accomplishing by not being somewhere else?"

"Meaning: who took your driver's license and my registration? A fascinating question. But I think we had better get out of here first."

The man behind the desk, while managing to convey that he was in no way mitigating the severity of Kate's misdemeanor, spoke to Reed as though he was now assured of not having an escaped, if harmless, lunatic on his hands. "Very well," he said, "we'll release Miss Fansler, provided she does *not* drive. You, I trust, have both an operator's license and a registration for the automobile you are driving?"

"Certainly," Reed said, reaching for them.

"All right." His glance was perfunctory. "You'll want to drive round to the garage that has the other car. Perkins, tell this gentleman where it is."

"I have a card," Kate said. "Is there a fine?"

"There will be. And you'll have to send your license in to have the convictions recorded, if and when you find it. In case you don't find it, you'll have to apply for another, and be certain to report the convictions. Good-bye."

"Oh, Reed, was I ever glad to see anyone? You may not feel in your element treading through cow dung or clinging to tractors, but in a police station, you're the man of my dreams."

At the garage, the mechanic, waving the generator, greeted Kate. "Someone pulled the wires out," he said. "Disconnected it. A kid's trick. I thought the brushes couldn't be gone after nine thousand miles. Look"— he waved the generator at Reed—"not even any corrosion on the armature."

"What would have happened," Kate asked, "if I hadn't had to slam on the brakes for that car?"

"Sooner or later, after you turned on your lights, the engine would just have died on you."

"But those wires must have been pulled out before I started. How could I have got this far?"

"There was enough juice in your battery to start her

up. With just the engine running, you'd go O.K. But your lights draw on your battery."

"Clever; very clever. I'm sorry about your generator, Reed."

"It's all fixed," the mechanic said. "I'll just screw it back in. Shouldn't give you any more trouble. Lucky I happened to be here."

"How much do I owe you?" Reed said.

"Six dollars, three for the labor, three for the towing."

Reed handed over the money. "The question is," he said, "how are we going to get this bug home? It will almost go in the back of your brother's car, but not quite."

"I could drive it, Reed. I'd be really careful, and now, with the generator back . . ."

"Perhaps I should have left you in jail. We'll just have to come back for it. Would it be possible," he asked the mechanic, "for me to leave it in your lot over there?"

"Help yourself. But I'll be glad to sell you a towline if you want to pull her home."

"Is that legal?" Reed asked.

"Not on the Taconic. Take 22."

"I guess it'll be cheaper in the long run," Reed said.

So it was rather with the air of being a procession that they arrived home in Araby. The household, including Leo, who had refused to go to bed, and who was suspected of hoping to see his aunt in jail, all came out on the lawn to greet them.

"And you said we never had adventures," Grace said.

"Some adventure. I was made to look like a perfect fool, never got to New York, and have exposed poor, much-beset Reed to even more Galahad-like endeavors."

"He always seems to be hauling one of us out of jail," William said, "but I still don't see what you did wrong."

So they all went inside to discuss it over refreshments, Kate, like Pooh, feeling the need of a little something.

"It's all very funny," Kate said to Reed later, when the others had finally gone to bed, "and doubtless it will make a lovely story in several years' time, like all those dreadful things that happen to Cornelia Otis Skinner that she manages to be so hilarious about, but what I want to know right now is . . ."

"Who was interested enough in your not getting to New York to go to all that trouble?"

"Suppose the state police hadn't come along? They might never have found out I was driving without a license."

"If you stopped anywhere along a parkway, they were bound to find you. But if by some chance you'd ended in a garage, even if you found someone who understood a car's electric system—and at that hour, most gas stations have only boys who fill tanks and wipe windshields—all of that would have delayed you sufficiently. Why?"

"It can't have been too serious a reason. I mean, the person clearly wasn't prepared to take life-and-death measures. He didn't fiddle with the steering mechanism, or the brakes."

"Kate, my darling."

"Oh, it would probably have been better if he had. I'd have landed in a ditch and gone on to take the train. I suppose everyone in Araby knew I was going to New York?"

"Did they know you were going to talk to someone at Lingerwell's firm?"

"Everyone in the household knew, I suppose. Somehow, in the country, everyone *does* know everything. Or maybe it's just that I'm not used to living in a household."

"Everyone in the house and: Mr. Mulligan."

"Blimey, yes. And Calypso's his publisher. Reed, do you think . . ."

"I think we had better sleep on it. Tomorrow I'm going to drive to New York, in brother's limousine, without telling anyone about it, and see Ed Farrell at

Calypso myself. Of course, it may all have been sheer malevolence."

"Let me go with you."

"Certainly not. You must wait here to come and rescue me when I get picked up for vagrancy. Anyhow, I hope to go and come in a day. You'll just have to drive Mrs. Monzoni in the bug without registration."

"Don't you think Ed Farrell is likelier to talk to me than you?"

"My title, such as it is, may go further toward convincing him this is a matter of great importance."

"Meaning, you can bully better."

"Meaning, whatever it is he has to tell, it may be betraying a confidence. There is, somehow, something more palatable about doing that to a lawyer whose interests are strictly professional."

Early in the morning, Kate heard Reed's car pull out. Deciding to get up and dress, she was not unbearably surprised to find, on opening her underwear drawer, her driver's license and the Volkswagen's registration reclining neatly on top of a pile of bras.

13

A Mother

After breakfast on Wednesday, Kate decided that, whatever the rites and rituals of rural life, simple kindness urged a call upon the young lady now holding up, so to speak, the pillars of the Bradford household. Undoubtedly, Kate thought, there was something she could do; if no act of neighborliness were discoverable, she could at least provide sympathy and an assurance of help at any future time, should it be needed.

Emmet, instead of immuring himself in the library, as was his inevitable wont, had taken himself off on a hike across the fields, an undertaking so atypical as to suggest an aberration. Still, there was no doubt, no one, since the murder, was really behaving a bit like himself. William, having taken Leo to camp, had continued, with Kate's permission, to Williamstown, where he intended to consult some books in the Williams College library, the nearest respectable collection of literary and scholarly works. From time to time Kate thought, rather desperately, of Reed's money, subject to forfeiture should William disappear altogether. Yet it did not seem either possible or desirable to restrict his movements. He knew the situation, and if his own sense of honor would not keep him from fleeing, certainly no external restraints were likely to.

Lina and Grace Knole were supposedly at work or, at the least, at thought. Lina, with her career yet to make, was working on a book to do with the proper names in eighteenth-century novels—an abstruse enough topic, yet not quite as firmly in the "how many angels can stand on the head of a pin?" category as the ordinary mocking layman might think. Lina was a brilliant teacher, alive, interesting and interested, deeply devoted to her work and respecting herself for doing it; but these qualifications were, these days, insufficient without publication. That no one but other scholars would ever read about proper names in the eighteenth century was not held to be an argument against the book, nor should it be. Still, how far had the subject chosen Lina, as subjects should choose those whom they overmaster, and how far had Lina arbitrarily decided on the subject since a book there had to be? Soon the whole profession would be swamped in an avalanche of published, unreadable works, neither conceived with excitement, nor nurtured with love, nor welcomed with gratitude.

Which recalled, of course, Grace's proposition of the night before. Might a college president actually reverse the trend, or at least run counter to it, making teaching, rather than research, again an honorable profession? Walking down the road, kicking at the gravel, Kate willed herself into a refusal to consider the offer of the presidency. Not yet, at any rate, was she ready to consider it. The brown dog trotted up. Kate greeted him, pulling his soft ears affectionately. "Reed's gone today, old chap," she said. As to Reed . . .

Kate had at least learned enough about rural ways to know that one never knocked at the front door unless one had been invited formally, and not always then. She walked around to the kitchen door and tapped on the pane. A young, pretty girl opened the door. Neither her age nor her looks seemed of first importance in any consideration of her because of a quality which was so clearly hers in amplitude: sweetness. It occurred to Kate, stepping into the neat kitchen, how rare a quality it was, how often its appearance was merely a cover for passions of an unusually hostile sort.

"How nice you've made the kitchen look," Kate said. Mary Bradford had talked constantly about how hard she worked, how none of her family ever put anything away, but her kitchen, her house, had always looked like Pandora's box, constantly pouring forth its unattractive contents. Now the working space in the kitchen had been cleared off; flowers, which Mary Bradford had never had time to gather, stood on the table. The girl had been about to make a cake using, Kate noticed, real ingredients—butter, sugar, flour, eggs—not a prepared mix, as Mary had done.

"I'm Kate Fansler from up the road," Kate said. "I should have come along sooner to offer my help, but somehow . . ."

"It must have been very hard," the girl said, "having all the confusion and nastiness of a shooting. Are the police gone?"

"Quite gone, I think, at least for now. The autopsy held no surprises; the arraignment of the young who fired the gun, while disagreeable, was not surprising either. Wouldn't you like to send the children up to us and have a few hours to yourself? You must have been working very hard."

"It's mostly been the visitors. Today at least they haven't started coming in the morning. But I do expect them this afternoon. I like people, really, but . . ."

"But not when they ooze four parts maliciousness to one part curiosity. And now I've come and ruined your one free morning. Why not let some of us sit with the children tonight, and you can go to a movie. Perhaps Mr. Bradford would like to go too. Let's take it as settled then. Don't let me keep you any more, now. If you should decide you want a few hours . . ."

"Please don't go, Professor Fansler."

"Goodness, no one calls me that, except a few students and book salesmen."

"Dr. Fansler, then."

"Absolutely *no one* calls me that, if I can help it. I'm always afraid of being asked to set a leg. Just Kate will do, or Miss Fansler, if informality makes you uncomfortable."

"Miss Fansler, a lot of the people who have stopped in have had a good deal to say about you, as I suppose you realize. That's how I knew you were a professor, of course: gossip. But Mrs. Monzoni says you're one of the few people she's ever worked for who trusts other people to go about their own jobs, and I imagine you've had a great deal of experience with people as a teacher."

"Some," Kate said, since this seemed to require an answer. "But I'm not very good at ladling out sympathy. I try to respond as sensibly and forthrightly as I can, but to tell you the truth, I'm not the motherly type. Of the students who don't like me, and their numbers are legion, half say I'm as hard as nails and the other half that I'm cold as a fish. They're probably right."

"You seem to me to be kind, and intelligent and sensible and able to keep things to yourself, and I simply don't know what to do," the girl said, and burst into tears.

"Blast," Kate said. "I am sorry. Can I offer you my handkerchief, only slightly used to get something out of my nephew's eye? The great advantage of country clothes is that they contain pockets, which city clothes, of course, never do—unless some dress designer has undergone an inspiration, and then the chances are ten to one he's put the pocket in such a place you can't put anything in it without looking as though you were starting a tumor—look here, Miss, I don't even know your name, but whatever the problem is, I'm certain it can't be as terrible as you think. Certain things, incurable diseases, are terrible—but most things only need to be expressed and they start getting into proportion. 'Troubles told are troubles halved,' as someone said, and if his little aphorism does sound simpering, it's nonetheless true for that. What *is* your name?"

"Molly."

"Look, Molly, if you've had the perception to see that I have an honest face, you've obviously got powers above the ordinary, and might as well take advantage of it. I don't gossip, or care especially about making trouble—my sins lie in quite other directions —so if talking will help, allow me to offer my ear. Don't you, by the way, think you ought to do something with that lovely mixture there? I've never made a cake in my life, but ought the milk to be soaking into the flour in those funny little channels?"

Molly smiled and turned on the electric mixer. "It will sound awfully foolish to you," she said.

"Probably. You'd be amazed how few human deeds don't sound foolish. My own follies are innumerable. With a girl as young and lovely as you it must be either a man or money; which is it? And you may not realize it, but if you plan to tell me you'd better hurry up about it or I'll begin sounding like a character in a bad play."

"I'm going to have a baby."

"I see. Mr. Bradford's baby?"

"Yes. How did you know?"

"People often make the mistake, Molly, of thinking that one learns nothing from books. One learns a great deal, actually. You're obviously in love with him. How pregnant are you?"

"Oh, I don't want an abortion, if that's what you mean?"

"That is not what I mean. I was simply wondering, as they say in bad plays, how long this has been going on."

"I met Brad first at auctions—my father is one of the main auctioneers in the county, and I used to go with him. Farmers' auctions, I mean. At first we only talked, but then—well, we knew we cared for each other."

"You must have met somewhere besides auctions, though admittedly my only experience of auctions is Parke-Bernet, where . . ."

"We did go out for meals sometimes, or for a drive. But we didn't, nothing happened, of course. He was married."

"And continued to be until he became a widower, what is it, four days ago? You can't have discovered you're pregnant in that amount of time. Now you know what is meant by 'hard as nails.' "

"You're right. If a man's married, it doesn't make any difference how he feels about his wife, or what she does."

"I wouldn't go that far. Frankly, Molly, I met his wife, and I should think that even the archangel Gabriel would forgive her husband for taking love anywhere he could find it, let alone with anyone as sweet as you. If I sounded harsh, it's because I've become a little sensitive about self-righteousness this summer. I'm sorry."

"You've just about said it, the way we felt. The reason we—it happened, finally, was because Brad said —he said she'd been unfaithful to him."

"Mary Bradford! I don't believe she could have stopped talking long enough. Is it possible?"

"He said—I'm afraid this sounds terrible. Brad said she'd only have done it if she was certain she could make two men absolutely miserable while she was at it. Him and the other one."

"I see. Incidentally, didn't all the years Brad has spent inseminating cows teach him anything about where babies come from?"

"That was my fault. Brad got me pills. But . . ."

"But you forgot to take them, one or two days." Molly hung her head. "You know, my dear, there's nothing like wanting to get pregnant by a man to whom you're not married to increase fertility. I wonder it hasn't been looked into more. It's the same principle by which married women who can't conceive al-

ways manage it the minute they take a job, return to
school, or plan a trip to Europe. Well, marry Brad
and have the baby. I'm morally certain you'll be a
better mother to his other two than the late departed."

"Don't you see," Molly said, pouring the batter into
cake tins, and then putting the tins in the oven,
"everyone is sure to say he murdered his wife. They
won't be able to prove it, I guess, but why shouldn't
Brad have put the bullet in the gun? He knew all
about guns, and he knew all about their pretending to
shoot."

"How did he know that?"

"The little boy told him."

"Leo?"

"Yes. He and the young man who takes care of
him, they used to come down to see Brad, and ride on
the baler, or in the hay wagon. Brad told me the boy
loved riding in the hay wagon and dodging the bales
as they were thrown in. I'm sure the boy—Leo—
didn't mean to say it was Mary they were shooting at,
but I'm sure he did. Anyway, Brad told me about it."

"I must be a very inattentive aunt. I didn't even
know Leo was riding in the hay wagon. It sounds
rather dangerous, dodging bales of hay. But then, William was supposed to . . ."

"We can't go on living here if everyone thinks Brad
killed his wife. And he didn't, Miss Fansler. You've
got to believe that. Brad wouldn't."

"Molly, let me give you one piece of ponderous advice. Never worry about what people think—people,
that is, whom you don't care for and whose opinions
you don't respect. And the odd thing is, once you stop
caring what people say, they largely stop saying it. I
don't deny it may be hard on the children if you stay
here with this murder over your heads—but anywhere
Brad farms, the story is bound to turn up, so why not
face it out here? There is, you know, always the
chance that they will find out who really put the bullet
in the gun. Live your life. Marry Brad, love his children, all of them, and stop paying attention to people
who aren't worth ten seconds' thought."

"I feel better. You won't tell anyone what I've told you."

"I don't promise that. I will almost certainly tell Mr. Amhearst, who is, so to speak, working on the case. But trust me not to tell anyone who isn't capable of keeping a confidence. Mr. Amhearst, by the way, is as likely to start gossiping with the neighbors as I am to become Shah of Persia, so don't brood about it."

"Will you have a cup of coffee?"

"Thank you. And then I must get back and join my guests for lunch."

"Please wait till the cake's finished and take it with you."

"I mustn't wait that long," Kate said, glancing at her watch, "but if you really want to make Leo madly happy, and send us all off our diets, we'll pick the cake up when we come to sit with the children, say at seven?"

"I'll send the cake up this afternoon. Don't think about sitting with the children, Miss Fansler. I like it here. I don't really want to go out anywhere at all."

"That's so obviously true, I won't urge you. When Leo comes home, I'll send him down for the cake. Will you promise to let me know if there's any practical way I can be of help?"

"Miss Fansler, do all your students burst into tears at the sight of you and tell you all their troubles."

"Only the few who notice my heart of gold beneath the rough exterior. Don't fret, Molly, it's not good for the baby. I'll stop in again in a few mornings, and we'll confine our conversation to the weather, if that happens to be all you feel like talking about. Thank you for the coffee."

It's all very well, Kate thought, scuffing her way back up the road, but what a motive! And who, after all, knew more about guns than Brad? His one defense might have been that he didn't know those two idiots were shooting at his wife, but Molly's now told me he did know. Can anyone be as innocent as she is and not be innocent? It would require a kind of doublethink I refuse to believe her capable of. What a ghastly mess. If Brad did do it, we can never prove it. It'll hang over his head all his life, and over William's head as well. But what way out is there? We are scarcely likely to find any hot clues now. If this were happening in one of those marvelous books by Ngaio Marsh, we would reenact the whole thing, starting with Saturday morning, and in the course of it the guilty one would give himself away. But I fear that's beyond our powers. Inspector Alleyn's methods are no doubt fine for Scotland Yard, but here in Araby it would merely seem as though we'd all gone crackers. Damn Reed. Why isn't he here to discuss this with me?

Reed, at the moment, was walking the pavements of New York musing, astonishingly, upon the breeze-swept meadows of Araby. The pavements seemed actually to absorb the heat and send it forth, many times increased. But the offices in which dwelt Calypso Publishing were air-conditioned. The receptionist who greeted Reed added her own coolness to the atmosphere, as though she suspected him of trying to offer her a lengthy, hand-written, unsolicited manuscript. When she learned that he wanted to see Mr. Farrell, her general suspicion of authors became visibly transmuted into a particular suspicion of salesmen.

"Do you have an appointment?" she asked.

"Not. Will you be good enough to take in my card, and tell Mr. Farrell I would like to see him on a matter of some importance?"

"Have a seat," she said. "I'll see." She returned shortly to announce that Mr. Farrell was on the long-distance telephone, but would be out shortly.

Ed Farrell, when he appeared, turned out to be a tall, handsome graying man of troubled mien. Reed got the impression that he spent many hours sitting up with authors, and was glad to see someone not large with book. "You haven't *written* something, have you?" he asked, as though unwilling to take Reed's nonwriting status on faith.

"I haven't even written a letter since my mother died five years ago," Reed said. "Thank you for seeing me. I'll try to be as quick as I can."

"What's the district attorney's office investigating now? Salacious literature? We don't print it."

"As it happens, Mr. Farrell, I'm here under false pretenses, and I had better tell you that straightaway."

"You're not an assistant district attorney?"

"I am, yes. But there's nothing official about my visit to you. In fact, I'm on vacation, and was on an assignment in England before that, so I haven't been near the office in months. On the other hand, this is not entirely a private matter either. It concerns a murder."

"You fascinate me. I don't read mysteries, though we publish, I am told, some of the best. In fact, I agree with that brainy critic who didn't care who killed Roger Ackroyd. But none of us, I imagine, is above the thrill of murder in real life, particularly if we don't know the victim."

"I'm staying in the country with Kate Fansler. A woman was accidentally shot near the house, by one of her houseguests. We have reason to think that the shooting may not have been as accidental as it looked —that is, that someone loaded the gun, knowing that it would be aimed in the belief that it was not loaded."

"How extraordinary. I know Kate, of course. Sam Lingerwell left all his papers to his daughter, and Kate's helping her look over them. Don't tell me you think she shot this woman. Kate's incapable of killing anything but a mosquito. She's even a great defender of spiders, whom she insists on calling our friends. Kate's all right, isn't she?"

"Fine, at least, as far I know. But interestingly enough, she set out last night on her way to see you."

"Really? I never heard from her."

"Not unnaturally, since she didn't get to call you. Her car was tampered with, and the license stolen; she ended up in a police station."

"She's not in jail?"

"No. We prevailed on the officer in charge to be

merciful. I want to ask you this, Mr. Farrell. Did anyone call you last night and urge you not to reveal something or other to anyone, under any circumstances?"

Mr. Farrell looked at Reed as though he had at last been granted a vision of the Delphic oracle. "Did you tap the telephone line?" he asked.

"Of course not. Can I persuade you to answer my question?"

"In a general sort of way, yes, considering your position and that you're a friend of Kate's. Someone did call last night, though not until rather late. I wasn't within reach of a phone till I got home about eleven. Maybe a little before."

"And he reached you then?"

"Yes. Always accepting 'he' as a pronoun applying to both sexes."

"Did he mention that he had been unable to reach you in the afternoon?"

"Yes."

"What I want to know, Mr. Farrell, is what that man, for I think it was indeed a man, said to you. I give you my word, as a lawyer, a district attorney, a man, and incidentally a friend of Miss Fansler's, that the information will not be used, or made public, unless it becomes essential to the solution of the murder. And in that case, I feel certain you would not consider it proper to keep silent after all."

"You put me in a very difficult situation, Mr. Amhearst."

"I'm aware of that, and believe me, I'm sorry. Kate seems to think a lot of you, and of course, as you know, she thought the world of Sam Lingerwell, whose firm you are now the head of."

"Only editor-in-chief of the trade department."

"Kate seems to think that you're the one who matters."

Mr. Farrell stood up. "Will you excuse me a moment, Mr. Amhearst? I'll be right back." He went out, shutting the door behind him, leaving Reed to look at the bookshelves, filled with books published by the

Calypso Press. It occurred to him, not for the first time, what an extraordinary human endeavor a book was. Mr. Farrell returned in fifteen minutes.

"All right, Mr. Amhearst, I'll talk, as they used to say in the movies when I was a boy. I've told them not to interrupt me with any calls, and to put off my appointment. Oh, never mind, just some hungry young idea man with a book that will sell in the thousands and not add one cubit to human stature. I went out to check on you. Anyone, after all, can have a card made up, or steal one, and know Kate Fansler, or say he does. Also any sort of man could be an assistant district attorney. We have a book of memoirs being done for us now by Justice Standard White, who used to be on the Federal Court of Appeals."

"I worked for him at one time."

"So he informed me, though I had only hoped he would have heard of you sufficiently to give you a recommendation. I've always thought it a great pity that he was never appointed to the Supreme Court, but no doubt we can discuss the vagaries of American justice on another occasion. He said he would trust you with his most treasured secret, should he have one. I also asked him to describe you. I may not read spy stories for pleasure, but one need only read the newspapers to know the odd things that happen every day, including impersonations."

"How did he describe me?"

"He said your clothes were Brooks Brothers, your manners Groton, your ideas Stevensonian (Adlai, that is), and that you looked like an extremely attenuated Trevor Howard with glasses."

Reed laughed. "It ought to be a very good book when he gets it written."

"So we believe and hope. Now, as to our problem."

"Perhaps I can simplify your unwelcome task by saying that I'm virtually certain the man who called you was Padraic Mulligan. What we can't imagine, frankly, is what he's got to conceal. I gather, from what Kate tells me, that he isn't the greatest writer of literary criticism since Matthew Arnold, but supposedly anyone could find that out by reading his books."

"That's the understatement of the century. He pours out books on modern fiction—'modern' being for him an elastic term to cover any work since Shakespeare he feels like mentioning—and makes a great many generalities about modern chaos together with plot summaries."

"Kate says he writes with some felicity."

"Ah," said Mr. Farrell.

"Do you mean he doesn't write his own books? You'd think he'd find someone at least competent to write them for him."

"Oh, he writes them, all right. At least, nobody else does."

"Mr. Farrell, you intrigue me. Has he blackmailed someone in the firm? Not you, I hope."

"It's hard these days to blackmail anyone who's heterosexual and hasn't actually left evidence of a major crime. That is, if that's what you mean by blackmail. Actually, he has blackmailed me, though the word is perhaps a trifle harsh. Book publishing *is* a business. Tell me, Mr. Amhearst, Justice White described you as a man of few frivolities. I gather that you read every word in the *Times,* enjoy an occasional decorous evening at the Plaza, and go to the movies and theater from time to time. Have you heard of Frank Held?"

"You don't have to be wildly frivolous to have heard of him. Like having heard of the Beatles; one can't help it. I've seen some of the movies about him —all naked women and complicated gadgets. I particularly enjoyed the one where the girl . . ."

"I see we're on the same wave length. Perhaps you know what those books bring in, what the reprint rights bring in, what the movie rights bring in? Publishers make a fair amount on best sellers like the Frank Held books, but that just makes up for all the good books they publish that barely make their get-out. The money really begins to come in, Mr. Amhearst, with subsidiary rights—movies, and so on."

"Interesting. But what has this to do with Mr. Mulligan?"

"He writes the Frank Held books."

Reed's surprise brought him to his feet.

"A *very* attenuated Trevor Howard," Ed Farrell said.

"The Frank Held books are written by an Englishman, what's his name. I know he hates publicity, and there aren't supposed to be any photographs of him, but the facts are plentiful enough. Why, I thought everyone knew he was related to . . ."

"Padraic Mulligan writes the Frank Held books. Believe me, Mr. Amhearst. And he was especially anxious that Kate not know it, and especially that someone named Knole not know it. I don't know when he began to realize he could make us publish his 'academic' books, and so get him a fast promotion in the crazy publish-or-perish academic world. What I can tell you is that everyone in the academic world is so busy publishing, no one reads anyone else unless he's in exactly the same line of country, and then only to be certain he hasn't been anticipated."

"But why should Mulligan want to go on being an academic? What an extraordinary thing. With what he's making he could, he could . . ."

"The ways of men are strange, Mr. Amhearst. No one knows that better than an editor. Whether he has a deep longing to be part of the academic world, whether he really likes to teach, whether his whole delight consists in mocking for his own benefit the standard of academic judgments, whether he secretly thinks his books are good—who knows? All I can tell you is that if we hadn't agreed to publish his academic stuff, he'd have taken Frank Held elsewhere. And we could not bear, Mr. Amhearst, to see Frank Held go elsewhere. I know what you're thinking. Sam Lingerwell could have borne it. Sam Lingerwell wouldn't have published Frank Held in the first place, and that's the bloody truth. But he lived in different times. What with mergers, the gigantic cash payments to authors—don't get me started. I console myself with the thought that one Frank Held, and one dreadful academic book by Padraic Mulligan, support any amount of first-rate stuff, some of it even poetry—stuff that doesn't sell in ten years what a Frank Held novel sells in ten minutes."

"Mr. Farrell, I won't waste your time with euphemisms and subtleties. Do you think Padraic Mulligan would kill to keep his secret from being made public, or to stop himself having to pay for silence?"

"Naturally, the question in my own mind. We can never say with assurance, but I should doubt it. In the end there would be too much at stake. He treasures his secretive role, and he never spends a fraction of the money he makes, or rather has left after the government gets through with him; he's a bachelor, of course, and our tax laws really do make true the old saw about two living cheaper than one."

"I know," Reed said. "I'm a bachelor myself."

"But Mulligan likes just having all that money. He's not a bad egg, you know. He likes giving people things, he likes to know that he could walk into any store in the country that sold anything, and buy it. The knowledge is more important than the purchase. In my experience, there are two general attitudes toward money: the one that wants to have a million dollars, and the one that wants to spend a million dollars. Mulligan is in the first class. He wouldn't risk all that, I think, even if his secret were in peril."

"Yet suppose, as happens to be the case, that he didn't actually have to *commit* the murder. There's the beauty of it. You drop a little bullet into a gun, and then leave it up to chance. You don't pull the trigger, you can't even be certain the trigger will be pulled."

"I don't believe it of Mulligan, though you can't trust me; I may be simply protecting a valuable property. But whoever dropped the bullet in that gun was taking a long chance—not only that the gun wouldn't be fired, but that it might be fired at the wrong person. It might have killed a stranger, a child—I think Mulligan would have shied away from that. He's got more imagination than your criminal seemed to require."

"Thank you, Mr. Farrell. You've been kind and more helpful than you can guess. I promise to preserve Mr. Mulligan's secret if it's at all possible. It was he who tried to stop Kate on her way to you, or so we think."

"It would appear so. When he reached me on the phone he complained of not being able to get to me all afternoon and evening, and he swore me again to secrecy as though he knew I would be questioned shortly."

"He did his best to stop Kate without injuring her, and he succeeded. I wondered that Mr. Mulligan would know enough to disconnect a generator in that way, and know exactly the effects of the disconnection, but of course, that's the sort of thing Frank Held has to know."

Mr. Farrell shook hands. "My best to Kate," he said. "Tell her to come and see me when she gets tired of cows."

After lunch, Kate poked her head in the library to see how Emmet was getting on. He seemed sunk in thought, and when she spoke his name, he leapt to his feet like one suddenly possessed. "I don't know what's the matter with everyone today," Kate said.

"I was thinking."

"No kidding. About whose problems, yours, mine or Joyce's?"

"All of them, I guess. Kate, would you mind shutting the door?"

"Only," Kate said, "if you promise not to confide in me."

"I'm saving that for when I'm a good deal drunker. I'm always more amusing when I'm drunk."

"As someone pointed out, you only *think* you're more amusing."

"I've got through the 1930s. Lingerwell's letters, I mean. I've been going through each year trying to collect the letters by author—I've explained all that, but this time around I've been paying particular attention to the Joyce letters, which are only beginning to be organized. Of course, the folders are just lying here— I mean, this isn't a guarded room or anything . . ."

"Emmet, I have never heard you so incoherent. And I thought that there was no situation which would find you without the right words, the light words . . ."

"You sould like an advertisement for beer."

"Ah, that's better. You'd got through the 1930s letters—"

"I was reading each letter, you know, trying to give future students a rough idea of the contents—my excuse, of course, since they're fascinating and I couldn't bear not to read them. Toward the end they get easier to decipher because Joyce dictated them, his eyesight was failing. The one I read yesterday was an ordinary, pleasant letter to Lingerwell—they hadn't been writing as frequently, but suddenly, in the middle of the letter is a sentence. Let me read it to you." Emmet picked up the letter and began to read with difficulty. He cleared his throat several times. Kate suddenly knew how he must appear to the woman he loved. She had never seen the mask drop before. " 'Watch out carefully, my dear Lingerwell, for the next letter I write you. There will be a long envelope —we can only seem to find a small one today—and in it an attempt to thank you for your help.' "

"Is that all?"

"That's all. The letter goes on to say he's fine, delighted with his grandson, and so forth."

"What was in the next letter?"

"That's it. It's gone."

"It may have been something valuable. Sam Lingerwell took it out and put it somewhere else."

"I wonder. A lot of these letters are valuable, in a monetary sense. But he left them all together, intending, I suppose, to go over them someday. Kate, I've been reading all I could get about Joyce, and you know, in order to thank that woman who supported him in Switzerland, he offered her the original manuscript of *Ulysses*. She declined it. Do you think . . ."

"That could hardly be contained in what Joyce calls 'a long envelope.' Besides, I seem to remember it was bought by some famous collector for a handsome sum. It can't be that. Emmet, are you suggesting that the envelope has been stolen?"

"I don't know."

"If someone stole it, why not steal this letter too, which gives the show away?"

"That's just it. Someone was looking through here, and happened on the valuable envelope, but didn't have time to check through for other references."

"I think you're imagining things. Perhaps whatever it was, was too valuable to accept as a gift, and Lingerwell sent it back."

"That's what I thought. But there's a reference in a letter years later, which seems to argue against that. Apparently Lingerwell had sent some money to the Joyces, whether his own or money he'd collected isn't certain, because we don't have Lingerwell's letters. But this last one from Joyce, dictated of course, refers obliquely to Joyce's past gift; it says: 'If you do as I have requested, and I trust you as much as anyone, it will be thirty years before you can consider yourself repaid.' Sounds rather as though someone else worded it for him. Joyce was very sick at the end, wasn't he, and then there was the war."

"What idiocy to have come to Araby at all. I should have persuaded Veronica to present the whole mess to the Library of Congress and let it go at that. What could this gift possibly have been?"

"Have you read Harry Levin? I think I'll go for another walk. Kate, you might as well know, I've searched the house."

"Emmet!"

"I had to, every room, dodging people, sneaking into guest rooms—illicit nocturnal pussyfooting between bedrooms is nothing to it. I think I'll take up being a sort of Raffles; if only I looked more like Cary Grant, and less like Little Lord Fauntleroy. I found your driver's license, by the way."

"Thank you, dear boy, but I had already discov-

ered it. You *were* thorough. Emmet, what are you
suggesting?"

"Walking in the fields isn't *so* frightful," Emmet
said, "if you sidestep the cow dung and refuse resolutely to think about snakes. Brad is out baling again
—enormous amounts of hay those cows eat."

When Leo came home, Kate sent him down for the
cake. "Try not to drop it," she said, "and walk carefully. Watch out for cars." Why is it, she thought, that
we cannot restrain ourselves from flinging advice at
children, though we must all know in our heart of
hearts that they are incapable of paying the smallest
attention to it. Perhaps it's the modern way of fend-
ing off evil spirits. "Leo," Kate said, suddenly remind-
ing herself of something, "I understand you enjoyed
riding in the hay wagon when the baler was flinging
the bales in?"

"Now, Aunt Kate. It's not dangerous. I showed
William. An *inchworm* could have gotten out of the
way."

"Where was William when you were riding in the
wagon?"

"He was there, most of the time. Sometimes that
Mrs. Bradford, you know, asked him to help her with
something. She was a real—I won't say it, now she's
dead."

"And, Leo. Do you think you could carry this bottle of wine down to the young lady who made the
cake without dropping it either, or drinking any?"

Leo appreciated this final jest. "I'll probably swill it
to the dregs," he said. And he reeled off down the
road, pretending to lift the bottle to his lips, upending
it in the process. When I think, Kate said to herself,
that Lord Peter Wimsey wouldn't even let anyone
dust a bottle of wine. There's no question about it, we
live in parlous times.

14

A Little Cloud

"As far as I can see," Grace said, coming up to Kate, "there's nothing wrong with that little boy. Of course I'm a childless old maid, and wouldn't know."

"Aren't old maids usually childless?" Kate asked.

"You're not. You've got Leo."

"Only for the summer, thanks be. How's Lina doing?"

"Waiting for William to come back from Williams —what an uneuphonious sentence."

"My advice to her was to try to think less about William."

"Have you noticed how advice like that always seems to have the opposite effect?"

"Now that you mention it, I have. Grace, this whole business is getting more and more disturbing. Emmet now thinks that a valuable Joyce letter, perhaps more than a letter, has been stolen."

"Does he indeed?"

"You scarcely sound surprised."

"I scarcely am. You can't put all that temptation under the noses of three people whose academic careers depend upon the chance to make a publishing coup—and not expect trouble. 'Lead us not into temptation,' the prayer says."

"You're terrifying me. Which three people?"

"William. Mr. Mulligan. Emmet himself."

"Mr. Mulligan? He's already a full professor."

"I know. He'd still love to make a coup, I'm sure. As to Emmet, who knows when the letter was stolen, or when, so to speak, he decided to discover it was missing?"

"Grace, you shock me."

"For the second time in two days—not bad, for an aged, cast-off lady."

"You resent it like hell, don't you, being retired?"

"Like hell. I try to recognize that retirement laws are important; we must get rid of old fuddy-duddies automatically, to keep from breaking hearts. But I do wonder sometimes if the cure isn't worse than the disease—it so often is, you know, in academic life. Perhaps I'm an old fuddy-duddy and don't know it, but I really think I still have all my marbles, and they are quite a handsome collection of marbles by this time. Something too much of this. What about you, Kate?"

"I? Don't ask me for an answer about anything. Maybe I'm just waiting for this murder to dim with time—maybe I'm just lying fallow, like one of Mr. Bradford's fields. I'm getting old, Grace. Don't laugh. There's old and old."

"I had no thought of laughing."

"Reed's asked me to marry him. It just goes to show, we all fall apart in the middle years. The one thing certain about Reed and me was that we would never really matter to each other. Grace, if a man hasn't married before he's in his forties, I don't think he ought to marry. I mean, one can't take up marriage as though it were the violin—to fiddle with in one's off moments."

"Jung has a theory about human life I'm rather taken with. I know the Freudians all frown on him, but to a literary mind, or perhaps I mean a mature mind, he speaks of possibilities beyond those offered by the viscera. As I said, a childless old maid. At any rate, he thought that about age forty—a few years more, a few years less—a human being needed to re- make his life because, in a certain sense, he had be- come a different person. It was the unconsciousness of this which caused many breakdowns in middle age. Jung didn't believe in looking back to childhood sex- ual patterns. He believed in discovering who it was you were trying to become."

"Grace . . ."

"Don't argue. Think about it all, and we'll argue another time. I wonder if you didn't get involved in this peculiar summer because you knew this kind of stasis was somehow needed, the protection of the womb before birth."

"Some womb."

"A womb with a view, as a wit remarked. You can't stand still, Kate. You've got to keep going, and changing, or die. Remember Emmet's saying some are dead though they walk among us; others have never been born. Personally, not to change the subject, I've always found Simone de Beauvoir hard to take, largely, I think, because even past forty, she kept right on acting like George Sand."

"So Lina's been talking to you about my talking to her."

"We all of us talk a great deal too much. Here comes Leo, about to drop the cake. Will Reed be back soon? He's the only one around here who ever seems to *do* anything."

Reed returned a little after five, seemingly intent upon refuting Grace's compliment. He was met in the driveway by Emmet, and the two of them began strolling down across the fields, obviously deep in con- versation. After a time they headed back, and Reed, capturing Kate, took her for a long walk in another field. He explained about Mr. Mulligan, but seemed unwilling to assume that that mysterious gentleman was guilty of anything more serious than stealing Kate's license and Reed's registration and generator wire. Kate told him of her day: her morning with Molly, and Emmet's discovery. "Emmet has already told me about that," Reed said. "Tell me about your conversation with this Molly: all you can remember."

"I'm not Archie Goodwin, who has total recall."

"We ought to hire him in New York, whoever he is."

"He's got a very good job already."

"Well, just try telling it as though you were one of those boring ladies on a park bench. 'And then she said, and then I said,' you know the sort of thing."

"You want me to be boring?"

"To be honest, I doubt if you could accomplish it. But try."

Kate tried. She was surprised at how a conversation came back, once she began trying to recall it. Reed listened attentively. Then he wandered off, and Kate was not *really* surprised to see him again in conversation with Emmet. She had gone inside when Reed again captured her and led her out onto the lawn.

"Kate," he said, "will you do something for me and ask no questions?"

"Not unless you tell me what. I've had a trying day."

Reed lit her cigarette. "I'm going to make it far more trying," he said. "I want you to go with me to a drive-in movie."

"You must be mad."

"Leo, who after all has been undergoing rather a rigid schedule, deserves a treat. Emmet will come with us because he likes new experiences on which to try his wit. William will come because you will expect him to accompany Leo, and Lina will come because William is going. Whether Grace comes or not is up to her; we need not urge her, if she doesn't mind staying home alone."

"Are you suggesting we all go in one car? It won't be a drive-in, it will be a squeeze-in."

"I'll drive, with Leo next to me, and William next to him; in the back seat will be Emmet and Lina and you. Of course, Lina too may decide not to go, but I doubt it. Needless to say, we will again take your long-suffering brother's car."

"I'd like to know what's long-suffering about my brother. He's in Europe, the lucky bastard."

"My language was inexact. I should have said, your brother's long-suffering car. Remember, you think the idea of a drive-in is too exciting for words."

"Reed, I hope you know what you're doing; it seems to me the sad deterioration of a first-rate mind. What's playing?"

"I have no idea."

"Don't you think my enthusiasm might be a little more convincing if I knew what the picture was?"

"Certainly not. The chances are ten to one it will be something you would never dream of seeing, like Elvis Presley. Your line is that you've been overcome with a need to experience American culture, regardless of the movie."

"Reed, I will *not* see Elvis Presley."

"Yes you will. Be good, Kate, and do as I say. I'll buy you popcorn at the drive-in, *if* you behave."

To Kate's astonishment, her suggestion of visiting the drive-in after dinner, which sounded to her ears about as convincing as a recommendation that they all play a fast game of touch football, was met with enthusiasm and a burst of high spirits. Leo, of course, was largely responsible for this. Once the possibility of such an adventure had been mentioned, it became inevitable. Emmet so amazed Kate with his eagerness to see a movie from a car that she suspected him of having had too much to drink. William showed signs of wavering, but Leo's "Ah, come on, William," was enough for persuasion. Lina said that she too would come, partly perhaps to be with William, but mainly, Kate thought, because she was the sort who would always rather do things than not.

Grace flatly refused to consider the whole thing, even if Reed offered to take his Volkswagen to make more room for her. "Preposterous idea," she said.

"Looking at a movie through a windshield. I can't think how such an idea ever caught on."

"The boys at camp say you go there to love some-one up," Leo announced.

"Leo!" came out in so emphatic a chorus from Kate and William that they could only laugh. "What," Emmet asked, "would Mr. Artifoni say if he heard you?"

"We don't let him hear us all the time."

"If you want to know the truth," Emmet said, "I read somewhere that drive-in movies are attended mainly by families; the children come in their pajamas and fall asleep as the evening goes on. The parents drop them into bed when they get home. No need for baby-sitters, and the drive-ins provide bottle warmers and everything else needed for the care and feeding of the human young."

"The things you pick up," Kate said.

"Are you sure you don't mind staying here alone?" Kate asked Grace, when they were preparing to de-part.

"Absolutely certain," she said. "Mrs. Monzoni will be here for a while, but in any case I'm not the sort to worry. Mr. Bradford is just down the road, should I need assistance in I can't imagine what contin-gency."

"Well," Emmet said, "I for one am selfishly glad you're staying. Pussens hasn't been feeling well"—Emmet picked up the cat, stroking it—"and I feel much better knowing she won't be all lonely-byes. I hope you don't loathe cats, Professor Knole."

"Not at all," said Grace. "In fact, I welcome the chance to make the closer acquaintance of one. I'm thinking of acquiring a cat *and* a canary."

Emmet had been quite right about the drive-in. In all the cars Kate could see were families with incredi-ble numbers of pajamaed children. Kate began to have the direst forebodings about a generation brought up on late nights in cars, receiving, as it were, movies subliminally. The movie was called "Moon-something"

—Kate had already forgotten what—and had been produced by Walt Disney, thus confirming Kate's worst fears, since she had never really believed Reed would expose her to Elvis Presley. At least the movie wouldn't be too wildly inappropriate for Leo, which was a load off her mind. "I can't wait to see Hayley Mills get her first kiss," one popcorn-laden girl said to another, passing by. Kate sank deeper into the seat of her brother's luxurious car and groaned.

The movie turned out to be a not greatly edifying example of the sort of story she and Grace had been discussing: much derring-do and some mystery, all of it revolving (literally in the case of one windmill scene) around the most extraordinary adventures. The lovers—doubtless one should call them the ingenues —were very young. "It is necessary," Kate reminded herself, "to remember that fifty-seven percent of the population of the United States is under twenty-five." That Kate and her contemporaries found the throes of first love agonizingly boring as not likely to be of the smallest interest to Walt Disney, who knew well what he was about.

The picture, having achieved at least fourteen climaxes, seemed, by the sheer necessities of time, to be drawing to a close: at least the heroine was confronting a woman who kept a pet leopard when Emmet, perhaps driven by an association of ideas, mumbled something about finding out how his pussens was. He left the car—a departure to which no one but Kate paid the smallest attention. It seemed to Kate that no great amount of time had passed when he returned, clearly the bearer of great tidings: "My god," he said, "troubles never come singly. First his wife and now his barn. Thank heaven there were no animals in it, except a few calves, which he rescued. Grace says it started with a little cloud of smoke, but now the flames are probably visible five miles away—a barn packed to the rafters with hay."

Emmet had spoken in a strong whisper to Kate, and the others wrenched their attention from the movie only slowly. "You mean his whole hayloft's burning?" Leo said. "Emmet, William, Reed, Aunt Kate—" he appealed to them all, leaving the young heroine to be eaten by the leopard should it choose. "Let's go back and watch it burn."

"Absolutely not," said Reed. "We'd only be in the way, and a danger to the fire department.

"Of course," Emmet said, "we should stay right here. Grace said they have the road cordoned off. They're just trying to keep the house from catching— it's all they can do. All that hay, it's hopeless. Thousands of bales of hay . . ."

"We've got to go, you fool," William shrieked, punching Reed as though to awaken him. "Drive. We've got to get back. They've got to put out the fire —the hay can't burn, do you hear, it can't burn, *it can't burn*." By this time his screams were so loud they attracted attention from the other cars. There were stares, and shouts for quiet. "Drive! Drive!" William shrieked. "They have to save the hay. Merciful God." He leaped from the car and started racing across the gravel, shrieking.

"Come on, Emmet," Reed said. "Kate. Drive Leo home. Now. Lina, stay with her."

But Lina had dashed from the car after William. As Kate moved into the driver's seat and began to maneuver the car out, she saw Emmet and Reed catch up with William. One of the attendants was already running toward him, and as she pulled past, quickly, so that Leo might not see much, she heard the scream of sirens coming toward them.

15

A Painful Case

"You may say what you want about Mr. Artifoni's camp," Kate said, "but if it were not for those sessions with first aid and basketball, I would hardly know what to do with Leo these days."

"The entire point of camps," Emmet said. "My objections were not to Mr. Artifoni, but to his maxims, so banal, and so oft-quoted. Ah, Reed at last."

"Will Cunningham defend him?" Kate asked.

"Let me at least get him a drink," Emmet said. "Have you left Lina there?"

"She hoped they might let her visit him. They've sent for a priest too, someone for whom William has a lot of respect—a friend really, I gather. Thank you. I need this. Cunningham will defend him, though whether the charge will be different, or the defense much changed—nothing has been decided."

"They won't—they can't execute him, can they?"

"No. Cunningham will certainly not allow that it was premeditated murder. That's going to be tricky, since of course he did get hold of the bullet, but Cunningham's going to maintain he found it more or less at the last minute— I gather that's somewhere near the truth, or as near as we're likely to get. Cunningham says thirty years, as an absolute maximum."

"Thirty years!"

"Twenty, more likely; eight, with parole and time off for good behavior. And Cunningham hopes to get him psychiatric help—there may actually be a possible insanity plea, though, as the law reads, that's almost hopeless. It's ghastly, I know, but look at the bright side. William will be helped, and Emmet and Mr. Mulligan and Mr. Bradford and his children, not to mention Mr. Artifoni and the Monzonis and the Pasquales, will be cleared of all suspicion. And of course, Kate."

"Surely no one really suspected me?"

"Not especially. But it is just as well, if one has any sort of highly responsible position, not to have even a suspicion of murder hanging about one."

Kate glared at Grace, who continued to listen to Reed with an air of unshatterable innocence.

"I," Emmet said, "will forever have the shadow of vile deception hanging about me, as far as Leo is concerned."

"He simply could not believe the barn wasn't burning. He kept running hopefully to the window—really, small boys are ghouls."

"What would you have done," Grace asked, "if William hadn't reacted?"

"If our plot hadn't worked, you mean?" Reed asked. "Emmet was taking that chance."

"Suppose I'd gone to the movie," Grace said, "and Emmet couldn't have pretended to call me?"

"He would have pretended to reach Mrs. Monzoni, still held to the house by the fire."

"Go on, Reed," Kate said. "Sum it up. You know how to begin: 'The case as I first saw it seemed a simple matter of accident; but that was only as I first saw it.' "

Reed got up to refill his glass.

"You might have let me in on it," Kate said.

"It was bad enough counting on Emmet's histrionic powers; I didn't want to count on anyone else's. Not that I underestimate Emmet's talents for drawing-room comedy, but melodrama seemed rather out of his line."

"Besides," Emmet said, "any risk, even so small a risk as of appearing an ass, was mine to take. In a sense, it was my fault."

"It was all our faults," Kate said. "Lead us not into temptation, as Grace said. I ought to have thought more."

"The only real sinner," Reed said, "though doubtless we are all too thoughtless of one another, was the woman he killed. It at least provides me with some satisfaction to know that it was not the innocent who suffered for Mary Bradford's sins."

"Did you think from the beginning it was William?" Grace asked. "The obvious man to the police, I think you said."

"Not from the beginning, but soon after. The more I thought about it, the more I realized that only a maniac would have taken the chance of leaving a loaded gun lying about. And for all the reports of that early morning target practice, would anyone really count on that as a way to murder the woman? Even if they thought the chance worth taking, the threat to the boy, to all of us, was preposterously great. It was the judge's horror of the gunplay at William's arraignment that made me realize that. And then, it was always Leo who shot the gun. Why not this time, if indeed there had been a plant by someone else of which William knew nothing? However terrible a deed William did, he did not let Leo shoot that gun. He was incapable of that, of letting Leo commit the murder, however innocently. Yet it was the fact that Leo did not shoot the gun which convicted William in my eyes."

"That's why I wondered about it so myself," Grace said.

"I know. The difficulty was, of course, while I'd decided William had loaded the gun as well as fired it, there wasn't a ghost of a motive. The woman may have been a monster—I think we all agree that she was—but William had never laid eyes on her before. How could he hate her enough for murder? Reluctantly, I began to look about elsewhere for my suspect—and for a time lit, as Professor Knole did, I think, on Mr. Mulligan. Upon investigation, however, Mr. Mulligan's innocence seemed assured, almost absolutely."

"Shall we ever know about that?" Grace asked.

"Forgive me for being mysterious. I shall have to ask for amnesty there. However, when I returned from New York and had two conversations, one with Emmet and one with Kate, the whole thing suddenly seemed to fall into place. I ought to mention, incidentally, that it has only been my recent association with Kate, my nearness to her in the same house, that apparently allowed me to learn from her the leap of mind necessary to, for me, so uncharacteristic a construction of events. To my honor, I was beginning to think like a professor of English."

"Most gallantly put, dear sir. But though pleased with the compliments, I am still bewildered by your conclusions."

"Emmet had discovered something missing, something that a letter from Joyce to Lingerwell had mentioned. There was always the chance that Emmet had taken it himself—though again, it is to Kate's credit that she was a good enough judge of character to think that unlikely." Emmet glanced at Kate, who flushed. I have grown not one whit better at accepting compliments, she thought. Damn.

"It was Emmet who did most of the guessing here, but of course, being a literary-type chap, he was used to letting his ideas leap about illogically."

"It begins to come naturally, after you've read Joyce awhile. It's more an association of ideas than a logical sequence."

"Sounds like *Tristram Shandy,*" Grace said.

"Is like, in a way."

"Tell them how your mind went," Reed said. "I don't think I could do it justice."

"First of all, I'd been thinking about *Dubliners.* That's why I gave our funny policeman 'Ivy Day in the Committee Room' to read. You know, he saw right off the solution was in those letters, and when I told him I'd been working on Joyce, he wanted to know about Joyce. He wasn't at all slow, for a policeman whose mind in no way resembled the White Queen's. Then there was a sentence of Harry Levin's, I don't know what the grounds for it were—here, I better quote exactly: 'Mr. Bloom's day first occurred to Joyce as the subject for another short story.' Add this sentence to the fact of the lost document, and—well—it suddenly seemed possible to me that *Ulysses* had started as a short story for *Dubliners,* and that Joyce, who of course waited so many years for publication of his stories, meanwhile decided that *Ulysses* would be his masterpiece, and withdrew the story from *Dubliners* before publication. He kept it though, as he kept *Stephen Hero,* an earlier form of the *Portrait of the Artist as a Young Man,* and it was this manuscript, or so I believed, which he sent as a gift, the most valuable thing he had to bestow, to Lingerwell. But he wanted it kept from the public. Why? That's still anybody's guess. Maybe he wanted *Ulysses* read in its own right—Lord knows, that hope succeeded beyond even his wildest dreams, I'm sure of that.

"This, as Reed or any of you would have pointed out, was only the wildest supposition. I hadn't a breath of proof for any of it. But I began to wonder, suppose there was such a story, suppose William had stolen it, hoping later to be able to claim he had found it, where would he have hidden the story? Not, I was reasonably certain, in this house. Of course, I searched. But if the story were found in this house, little of the credit would be William's. Lingerwell's daughter would dispose of it as she would dispose of all the other papers. But if he could find it in a dramatic way, a way similar to many of the literary discoveries of recent years, he might be allowed to bring it out; at the very least, his name would be connected with it. But where could it be hidden?

"As you can see, I wasn't a bit closer to a solution, but I was beginning to think like William; suppose, I thought, I walked the fields as he did with Leo, would the hiding place strike me as it struck him? I thought at first he might have taken Mary Bradford into the plan and then have had to kill her, but that seemed too wildly improbable. There was absolutely no questioning William's loathing for Mary Bradford. Anyway, though I actually tramped over the fields, I didn't think of anything. But I did talk to Reed about the missing story and tell him my theory."

"Before you spoke to me?" Kate asked.

"Yes. I felt he was likelier than you to call me a fool. And I couldn't let you live with the possibility of such a theft unless I really believed in it. Ultimately I did tell you, though not that I suspected William. After that," Emmet said, shrugging his shoulders, "it's Reed's story."

"I grabbed the stick, so to speak, from Emmet's faltering hand. Not a bad image, really, for my purposes. I came to it fresh, a new runner. He was already tired. In the end, however, I too nearly dropped with fatigue until I started recapitulating my whole visit here—one of the most wonderful and dreadful visits I have ever paid—and I remembered my first morning, being instructed in and bounced mercilessly about on Mr. Bradford's baler. I remembered also that Mary Bradford had seen me out there. Remembering all this, I again walked across the fields, and as I was watching that machine forming a bale, it came to me suddenly how even a good-sized manuscript could be neatly hidden in one of those bales, if one merely dropped it into the machinery when Bradford was looking the other way.

"I thereupon asked Bradford, with what I fondly hoped was a careless air, if the machine would wrap a wad of paper up with the hay? 'That's the second time I've been asked that question in as many weeks,' Bradford said."

Grace Knole whistled. "What a hiding place. To hide a needle in a haystack."

"But, of course, one must have a chance of recovering the needle. I went on talking to Bradford, and discovered that William had approached him for a job as handyman, to begin work in September. He spoke of needing a job while working on his dissertation, of wanting to do physical work, and so forth. He knew of course how hard it is for farmers to find hired men these days."

"And he intended to 'find' the manuscript while working for Bradford. Ye gods, did Bradford hire him?"

"No. Bradford was rather circumspect here, but he *seemed* to be suggesting that he suspected William of having had an affair with his wife."

"So that was it," Kate said. "Molly said—but I never thought . . ."

"Naturally not," Reed said. "There's so much we can't know, and probably never will, though with luck and the grace of God, a psychiatrist or a priest, perhaps between them, may unearth it. I think she seduced him—perhaps out of sheer malevolence, or a mad kind of lust. All that is certain is that she saw him put something into the hay, and learned that it was something he treasured; her knowledge put him in her power. I can't believe he ever told her what it was, which is, you know, the saddest part of all. Because had she known it was a story, she probably would not have thought it worth bothering about. I'm certain she had never heard of James Joyce. God knows what she thought it was."

"For some horrible reason," Emmet said, "I imagine it was in that very hay, where his treasure was, that she made him make love to her. It must have been, if Bradford found them. Perhaps he wouldn't have killed her for either thing alone, the story, or the assault on his chastity. Or perhaps the thought of her leering at him as he searched, as he had to search, through that hay, was more than he could bear."

"Whatever way it was," Reed said, "when Kate recounted to me her conversation with Molly, the girl Bradford loves—it all fell into place. It explained Lina, it explained so much."

"And on that walk back from Mr. Mulligan's party," Kate said, "I thought he was talking about me. I should have known he would never . . ."

"Oh yes, it all fits, once you think about it. Emmet and I agreed. But there wasn't a shadow of proof, not a glimmer. And what Molly said to you, Kate, was truer than you admitted. Bradford would have been doomed with having murdered his wife in any community, considering the motive he had."

"So you tried your little act with the fire?"

"It seemed harmless enough. If it hadn't worked, we would have lost nothing but face—Emmet's face—and he was ready to risk that."

"Do you mean to say," Grace said, "that there is a priceless, unpublished James Joyce manuscript wrapped in one of thousands of bales of hay on the top of Mr. Bradford's barn?"

"Oh yes, it's there all right. William had the letter on him when the police took him away. He hid the manuscript but he kept the letter. It just said: 'Here it is, Lingerwell. Bloom's first appearance in print.' "

"I can't wait to read it," Emmet said. "Do you suppose Bloom was seen as part of the general paralysis, as in the other *Dubliner* stories, or was he already the apostle of love?"

"What I want to know," Kate said, "is what I am going to do with the four thousand bales of hay I have today purchased from Mr. Bradford. Where does one keep hay in New York City?"

"I only hope," Emmet said, "he starts today using some other hay for his cows. Can you imagine that story, that precious story, in the stomach, one of the four stomachs, of a cow, slowly being churned into manure or fertilizer? What a horror!"

"An event, nevertheless, which would vastly have amused Joyce," Kate said. "Read *Ulysses*."

Epilogue

The chairman of the James Joyce Society rose to speak.

"Ladies and gentlemen. The sixty-second anniversary of Bloomsday has passed," he said, "to be followed by an event so earthshaking that one could scarcely have conceived of anything so magnificent. Incredible though it may seem, a sixteenth story originally intended for *Dubliners* has been discovered. A story which may well have been the first to tell of Mr. Leopold Bloom. Here, to recount the fascinating details, is Mr. Emmet Crawford."

There was applause and many eyes glistened, most of them male. In the back of the room, unobtrusively seated, were a lady, a gentleman, and a small boy looking quite pleased with himself. Emmet Crawford arose.

"Thank you, Ladies and Gentlemen. We all share, I am certain, the same excitement. But, alas, neither I nor any of us has a new manuscript by James Joyce. We have only what is perhaps little more than a wild hope for a manuscript by James Joyce. What we have at the moment, ladies and gentlemen, is four thousand —no, let me be accurate, as Joyce would have approved—three thousand, two hundred and thirteen bales of hay!"